Echo of the Whip-Poor-Will

Return to High Falls

**When we were young
And not so very long ago**

© Don Hayward 2018

"Echo of the Whip-Poor-Will," by Don Hayward

ISBN 978-1-7752459-1-9 (Softcover)

Published 2018 by Don Hayward,
8 Huron Lane, Goderich, Ontario, Canada N7A 3Y2

Manufactured in Canada

Also by Don Hayward

Collapse
Book One of After the Last Day
ISBN 978-1-7752459-2-6 (Soft cover)

Under Shadows
Book Two of After the last Day
ISBN 978-1-7752459-4-0 (Softcover)

The End of shadows
Book Three of After the Last Day
ISBN 978-1-7752459-5-7 (Soft cover)

The Seventh Path
ISBN 978-1-62137-949-2 (Soft cover)

Journey's End
ISBN 978-1775-245933 (Soft cover)

Murder on the Goderich Local
ISBN 978-1-62137-993-5 (Soft cover)

Sherwood Green
ISBN 978-1-7752459-0-2 (Soft cover)

Return
ISBN 978-1-7752459-7-1 (Soft cover)

High Falls

A pictorial history

ISBN 978-1-7752459-6-4

All of Don's books, except High Falls, are available in an electronic version from Smashwords.com and Amazon (and soft cover).
The five collapse books and the science fiction are available through book sellers worldwide.

Contact Don,
haywardon@gmail.com

when we were young
and not so very
long ago when
the winter did not
sit upon the land but came flaunting
settling amongst the spruce
waiting silently five months
in the cedar swamp for the sun's memory

when we were young
and not so very
long ago when
the bush stopped
the pine rested cold and quiet
only shattered but little
when we stood in awe
as Dad's axe cut and echoed and splintered
a tree for Christ
praying with our excitement and hope
then leaving the others
sleeping silently, alone

when we were young
and not so very
long ago when
touch and smile kept us safe
and we were not alone
when we were young
and not so very long ago

-   Don Hayward

This book is a gift for all my family. May they one day find it worthwhile; may others find something of value here.

Dedication: To foster children everywhere, especially our Little L and R, who fate denied their "High Falls" to explore forever in memory. I hope they find cherished memories to comfort in the dark hours. To my family and friends from High Falls, may you forever hear the cry of the loon and the echo of the whip-poor-will.

Acknowledgement

Thank you to my wife Diane who gives her help and encouragement in this and every other endeavour. My life was a smooth, paved road compared to hers.

Thank you to Alex, for your patient reading and helpful suggestions and to my cousin Carol, who has been a source of information, support and laughter.

Thank you to the Sudbury Library Historical Collection for hard work in providing information and leads to pursue.

iv

Photographs

All photographs, except for where noted are from Don's work or the Hayward/Prentice collection, special thank you to my cousin, Carol Prentice Chepurny for many pictures and information that I may not have included but influenced the clarity of my memory and stimulated thoughts.

Cover: High Falls from the blueberry hill, October 1968–*Don Hayward*

Back cover: Sunset on Agnew Lake, August 1968–*Don Hayward*

Author's Word

I have based this story on my memories, but the melodrama is fictional. Any resemblance between those characters and real people, living or dead, is coincidental.

You may skip this section and go straight to chapter one; however, the map and satellite photo may help you understand locations mentioned in the text.

In the engaging stage play, Ipperwash, at the Blyth Festival Theater in Ontario, Falen Johnson and Jessica Carmichael lead us to consider place, loss of home and dislocation from our roots. They presented the story as an explanation of the native peoples' connection to the land. I left the Blyth Theater with a mixture of excitement and sadness in my heart.

Our industrial culture over the past 200 years has led to dislocation for most of us, as economics has forced people to move or has obliterated our places of youth, and in my case, both happened with High Falls. It had disappeared by 1986.

My experience in fostering children has taught me that life denies the opportunity for many young people to have a place of roots for happy, youthful memories. Perhaps this is the basis of the growing craziness of the industrial world.

Readers of my first fiction, the five books of the "After the Last Day" collapse thread, may recognize that this loss is one of the great shadows that dogged my characters. I cannot say we all yearn for the recovery of place, but I always have. I never really felt at home anywhere. This story explores my yearning.

I am presenting here a personal and incomplete vignette of my life in High Falls until about grade 10. At that age, High Falls changed from being my world, to become my sometimes refuge as I focused more of my life on outside interests, high school and university. In later life, High Falls has become my refuge of memory, my spiritual place that anchors while waiting for the call into the safe harbour. I left High Falls for the last time in January 1970.

High Falls is a hydro-electric generating complex built where, in a series of rapids and falls, the Spanish River descends over an ancient fault line in the Earth that we can trace all the way from Quebec to Montana and known in this area as the Murray Fault. Local faulting is a consequence of the asteroid impact almost two billion years ago that created the Sudbury basin. High Falls sits about 50 km west of Copper Cliff, Sudbury and 20 km straight line from Espanola which itself exists because of another falls on the river.

The reader can find the story I briefly outline below in more detail in my book, High Falls, mentioned above.

People logged The Spanish River valley extensively in the late 1800s, and a logger first suggested that the complex, then known as Twin Falls, would be a suitable site for electrical generation. The Canadian Copper Company created the Huronian Power Company, and the site generated first power in 1906. My grandfather, Albert Prentice, arrived in High Falls in 1912.

After 1906, Huronian completed the secondary dams for the lower plants and No. 2 generating station, making it possible to establish the town on a sand and clay levee east of the power plants. The river, about 200 meters wide, defined the southern extent of the houses, and No. 2 tailrace marks the western boundary. The swimming-hole beach lay near the lower rapids below the falls about a kilometre upstream from the village.

Until the 1930s, a spur from the Eastern Algoma Railway, later the Canadian Pacific served the site, and they named the junction "Turbine". Many workers laboured there in the era before diesel power could replace them, and at the height of construction, perhaps 3000 lived at the site.

The only traces of their camps were the trash heaps east of the town.

They completed Big Eddy dam in 1920, creating the 40 km long Agnew Lake, but the power plant did not generate electricity until about 1930. The Big Eddy dam is one and a half kilometres upstream from the town and No. 1 plant, first reached by a railway line and later by a road that paralleled the abandoned track bed. Water drops in two stages, almost 60 meters from the level of Agnew Lake to the High Falls tailrace.

I only knew the town long after the High Falls Road replaced the railway. In the story, you can trace this on the map and satellite photo below; I walk on the roads that follow the old tracks. I stop at the No. 2 plant near the ponds in the river bed left exposed by damming the second falls that gave the name "Twin Falls". Then, I reminisce at the west end of the secondary High Falls dam, a hundred meters off the Big Eddy road and across the High Falls No. 1 and 2 water intake canal from the "overflow" dam. After, I walk on up to Big Eddy. In the end, I sit at the spot about 30 meters above the town-site, where the old railway trestle brought the tracks up to the level of Big Eddy road, halfway up the big rock hill that dominated the northern side of the town.

Our school sat on the east side of town, just past the little creek. The gate is now just west of where the stream passes under the only road that enters the complex, although we had three ways into town. The low road went to the town and the high road to the power plants between the houses and the hill. A back road passed behind the school, through the edge of the bush and on to our house. The two main roads connected at the school and with two side streets, one between the clubhouse and Grandpa's house and the other between the clubhouse and the little cottage house where we first lived. Quietness dominated life, with little vehicle traffic and a lot of walking. As children, we walked or biked everywhere.

What we called the "sandpit" or "the hopper" was about a half-kilometre downstream, where the river made a sharp turn over a gravel bar and disappeared on its way to Nairn Falls and Espanola. The garbage dump was two kilometres out of town towards Turbine, which was about five kilometres from the village. The satellite photo and map on the next two pages show the overall layout.

Gone are the children
Simple pleasures and fun
Carried into adulthood
On times constant run

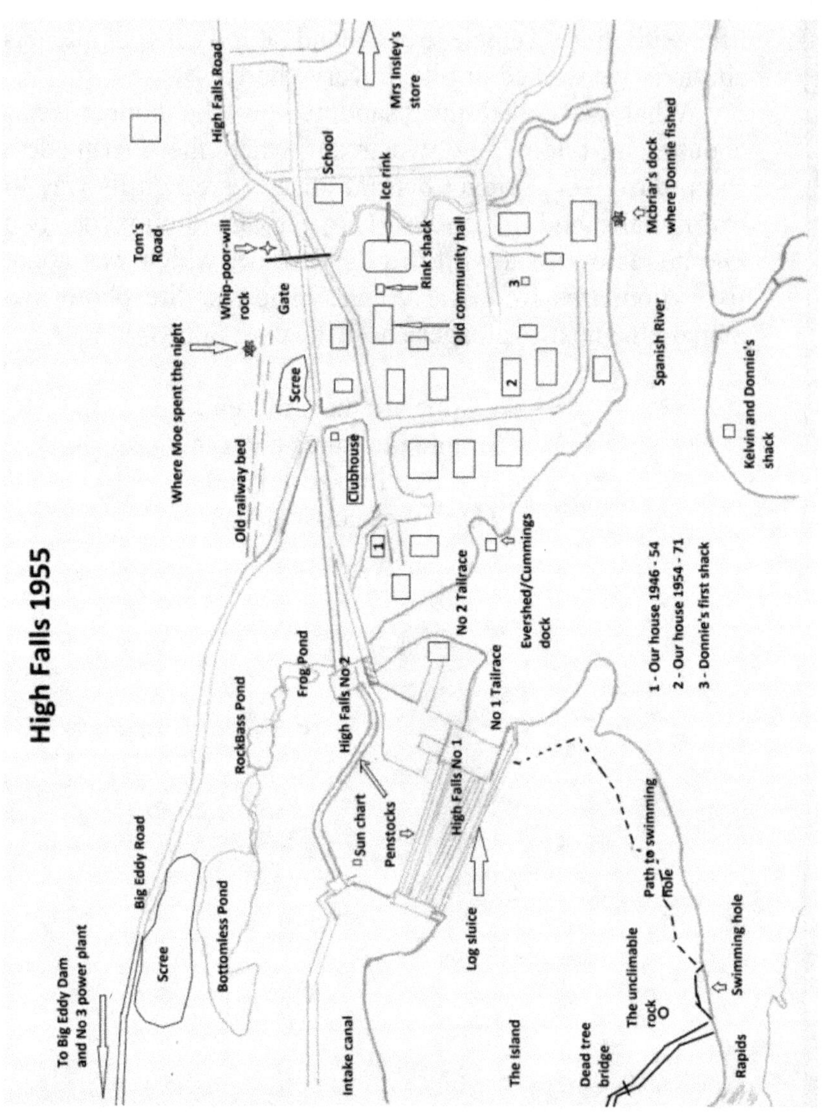

Fig. 1 Sketch map of the town-site, close to scale but approximate locations of buildings and points of interest in the story

A general satellite view of the complex in 2018 is courtesy of Google Maps.

At the outset, I had to struggle with how personal to be and whether to name the actual people I knew. I used real names where they came to my memory, and if there was a somewhat negative relationship, I stress that this account is from my point of view while others may have had another experience, which I did not understand or appreciate.

There is only one instance I use a made-up name. Despite the deep anxiety I felt from our earlier confrontations, in 1969 I worked beside this person, and we had a positive relationship. We both had changed. Tragically, the young man in question had his struggles with alcohol that suddenly cut his life short. I am still thankful our relationship taught me that healing and transformation are possible in human affairs. It seems to support the native's concept of healing circles and restoration. If there is a secondary purpose to this effort, it is to pass on that possibility for my children and grandchildren to consider.

I am not writing a "tell-all", so I will not pile on the personal angst but focus on the memory of mostly pleasant places and events. As well, it is not a story of continuous upward progress in maturing and understanding. Life is not like that but made up of the dialectical dance of advances leading to setback and then defeats, turning to victories in an endless cycle.

This story captures photographs from my memory that I had not put into photographs. I want to share these with family and perhaps other interested people. I am also trying to sort out memory and place in my mind and heart. The photographs in the document somewhat match the narrative.

I seldom write any story with a pre-conceived structure, but as a flow that grows naturally that I fix on paper. This account is the same, so memories, as they occur in the story, may not be in chronological or geographic order. These memories have frequently come to mind throughout my life and have the randomness of flashing signs in a streetscape. Readers may experience this confusion of time and space reflected in the simple literary device I employ, the interaction between Moe and Donnie. In part, this style is a tribute to the native way of preserving history through a story.

In the same way, the dramatic story is not only to add some interest but to remind us, especially me, that High Falls has changed and new people are living out different lives, writing fresh stories connected to the place.

The text reflects the randomness of our play as children in High Falls with no plan. One day we would visit the sandpit downriver, another up the big hill, and another to "the Island" between High Falls No. 1 and the falls, bike to the garbage dump, to the dams, frog pond, or Big Eddy. Summers especially held a random wild ride in a real-life natural wonderland. Each day was an escape into the orchard. We had so many apples to pick. Moe's explicit memories and Donnie's seemingly random adventures describe actual events and places in my childhood as accurately as I remember them.

These memories have always brought feelings of pleasure and longing. I hope the work summarizes these for my family, memories and thoughts that I sadly never fully received from my parents. I had no opportunity to hear from Grandfather Prentice, who disappeared from my life dying before I was two, or from Grandpa Hayward, whom I never knew but only a name and a photo of a middle-aged man. Grandma Hayward simply appeared as a weathered grave marker in Kettleby cemetery. I longed to know Dad's heart in his own story, but his experience pained too much for him to pass it on, and some of what Mom shared carried her pain.

In love, I give mine to you all.

Aspen, birch and pine
Blazing October
Colours this heart of mine
Setting feet restless
Upon memory's road
Visiting places that
Be no more
But living wild
Within this memory

-   *Don Hayward*

Chapter One

The car pulled off the travelled portion of the road, crushing small shrubs on the edge of a gravel turnout.

Pussy willow, Moe thought.

The vehicle stopped on flat ground with long grass and goldenrod all about. From a short distance, the car appeared to be floating on a prairie sea with ripe seed-heads waving in the breeze. Most would not have dared to park there, but the old man behind the wheel knew he had stopped in the old gravel schoolyard, hidden by the decades since they had torn the building down. He remembered when they had built the place the year he started Grade One. The most vivid memory was of what seemed like the huge "steam shovel" that made the waterline and the oakum and solder at the joints. The digging machine was neither large nor powered by steam.

Funny how memory works, thought Moe, *of all the little details I could have remembered. It is only that.*

Moe's eyes had not looked upon this spot in many years. His life had taken him far, around the world and then filled with family and love, but there had always been the emptiness, the memory of this place, the need to return, the desire, the longing.

It was a warm day, one of those September days that often came to mind when Moe thought of his old home.

Crimson and gold, blunted by the deep burnished colour of red oak in fall glory, ran up the hill as they always did, before the big storm later in the month stripped them bare.

He pushed the car door shut, felt the warmth of the sun on the maroon paint and looked up the hill, his hand shielding his eyes and reducing the watering that had become so common for him in bright light.

Moe usually treated his appearance carelessly. All his life, his clothes, his teeth, his hair had all seemed slightly off. The gap in his front teeth led to avoiding smiling, and when someone expected a smile, he forced it. He had always admired the easy, confident grins of others.

False teeth fixed that, Moe thought, and remembered the joke about how you could tell a hockey player at a party because they were the only ones with perfect front teeth.

His hair and beard had always been a dynamic adventure with Moe's appearance lately, cycling between Santa Claus and the retired civil servant look. Moe had never qualified for either job. Today he had felt it necessary to have a haircut and crop his beard to a tidy centimetre, with the moustache trimmed. He needed to look his best today, in keeping with the rest, had worn a fresh flannel shirt, and pressed pants, clean socks in new ankle-cut hiking shoes and clean underwear.

"You don't want them to find you in dirty underwear," Mom always said, no doubt passing on the Prentice women's slightly skewed opinion of the human body.

Going home perhaps, he thought, *or paying my last respects to a dead place.*

The deep colours of the scrub oaks still framed the hard grey rock, but all the trees were different, bigger and new, hiding most of the hill. It was familiar, but strange. He briefly wished that it were high summer, when he might later hear the whip-poor-will as dusk descended. An enormous boulder, the common roost for the shy night bird, sat at the base of the grey, granite hill and almost obscured by the trees and scrub that engulfed the meandering creek. The stream, hidden and full of memory, burbled from recent fall rain. The whip-poor-will always had sat on the rock, serenading High Falls into darkness.

Whip-poor-will; Whip-poor-will; Whip...

Moe looked away towards the place where his home once stood.

I can still hear the echo of the whip-poor-will behind me, making the town real or perhaps reminding me that High Falls itself is only an echo in my mind.

Whip-poor-will rock in 2014

Moe turned back to stare at the rock slope that had once been bare; with a few sumacs and a lot of thick rock-moss clinging to whatever fracture and ledge the last ice sheet had left and broken by the concrete footings of the long gone railway trestle. The voices of children at play seemed to echo still as they scrambled over the steep face, throwing clods of moss at each other while trying not to tumble down.

Luckily, no one ever got hurt. I wonder what that whip-poor-will thought while trying to catch some rest amid our nonsensical pandemonium. That grade-seven teacher used to take part, an educated Scot who had remained a child.

Moe had not liked the man, but, it seemed he might be the only one in the school who felt that. To Moe, the teacher had been a bully, humiliating Moe in front of the entire class by threatening to strap him for God knows what, and he allowed a bigger boy repeatedly to bully Moe. Not even Moe's older brother ever came to his aid during those humiliating attacks by Davie, and the child-like teacher had laughed.

My friend, Warren, before he died, told me how much he admired that teacher and how the man had opened Warren's eyes to the world. Of course, the teacher lived with the Eversheds, so Warren got to know him outside of school and saw a side of the man hidden from me. He gave good feedback on my Grade 7 report. Life is not simple.

Moe tried to recall how many kids from that pathetic one-room school had gone to university. It seemed an impossibly large number, and even more important, most of the kids had satisfying and successful lives other than through school.

It was the times, thought Moe, *expansion, optimism, a faith in intellectualism and everyone had a firm belief that as adults, they expected us to take care of ourselves. You could get a good job almost as soon as you were sixteen, even if you did not excel at school. Companies expected to train you on the job then, not dump that cost onto the school system.*

Chapter Two

An ugly gate with a video camera on a pole blocked the old road, what Moe called the "high road". Moe waved, but his image likely disappeared into the guts of some computer, unseen by a human. In his youth, before the voices of children on the rock had faded, until the company ripped the town into oblivion, no one had cared who passed here: workers, residents, relatives, miners coming to fish on the weekend, bear, moose… children.

Children!

He stared, wiped a small tear from his eye, and eased to the gate, the spot beyond where the road crossed the little creek. The bridge, built before his time, a solid concrete slab, had carried the railway over to the still standing generating stations. An ugly corrugated, galvanized steel tube, practical but not notable, now took the slab's place.

His hand grasped the wire mesh of the gate, and he rattled it, pulling hard.

"You damned thing," he shouted. An echo whispered from the nearby rock face.

Silly Moe, silly Moe, silly Moe.

This modern monstrosity mocked him, this contraption; this symbol of the fearful, possessive decay of the world, built against the lawsuits of people wanting to make a buck in any devious way.

The fence represented the fifty years since he last felt free here. The free roaming of the children in his day would now anger and frighten the powers-that-be, minions, mere functionaries of the corporations that lay on the land like caustic slime. He pulled back from the fence as if it had burnt his hand. The camera on a pole beside the gate silently watched, its large black eye focusing on Moe.

Moe looked down the creek to where the abandoned low road used to cross the stream. Originally, it had a wonderful old bridge made from salvaged railway timber with lots of little nooks beneath for youngsters to explore, cool, mysterious, scary with the chance of snakes, but with frogs and tadpoles. In time, they replaced the bridge with an ugly culvert, but they had removed even that. Moe remembered the thunderous flash flood of '67 ripped that pipe up and threw it downstream as if nature abhors the things. The torrent had not moved the concrete slab of the high-road bridge.

So much for modern innovation, he thought and turned to look up the road to where the old No. 2 power plant still stood.

No. 2 power plant from the gate

Unknown to Moe, his shaking had triggered an alarm 60 kilometres away. A bored security guard dropped her crime novel and focused on the monitors that showed *some old coot interfering with the High Falls fence.*

She dialled her boss and watched as the old man stared at the gate, but did not seem to do anything. The boss arrived, and they watched the screen. Nothing much happened.

"Keep an eye on him. Probably it's one of those old residents come for a look. Let me know if he trespasses."

She returned to her book, glancing at the screen from time to time. The old man stood motionless.

Moe's eyes travelled from the road to where the hamlet once stood. He stared for a long time, trying to remember exactly how it had looked with the neat white cottages and green-trimmed houses, the gravel road, the bare hill where the Insulbrick covered community hall had dominated; it had been the old school and a hospital before his time.

Mom taught there, one year, he thought, *and out at the Turbine school. John went to grade one in the old place the last year before the new school opened.*

And a church, Moe remembered and chuckled, *where I learned to whistle during a hymn. Whistling wasn't part of the United Church liturgy, and I did not impress Mom.*

The rink shack, made from an old police guard hut by the work gang, had sat below the hill near where the ice rink appeared every fall. When they were older, the kids would sit in the shack on the nights too cold to skate and tend a fire in the old woodstove, gossiping and laughing. Echoing children's voices stirred him.

Old community hall and rink shack, looking north from our backyard.

Moe remembered the hall, and the time they had taught their dog, Lucky, to climb a ladder onto the roof. The dog had all the bravery of the kids. They had put someone's wooden ladder up to the roof. Lucky followed, and Moe could still see him coming back down, bravely running head first and putting his paws on each board rung as he came. Moe had feared for him, but the dog seemed proud. Lucky often played with them as if a kid.

I wonder if they bothered to take the fence far down the creek.

Moe retrieved a small backpack from the car with water, a thermal blanket, and trail food. He found walking a chore but struggled through the trees, passing over the spot where his school desk might have sat, near the big west windows of the single classroom. Moe paused and looked west. He once sketched the town in fall colours, through the school window to break the boredom as the teacher imbued wisdom into some other grade. Tall, red pines still dominated the head of the island above No. 1 Dam. Thick trees obscured it all.

He remembered the first poem he ever wrote, sitting in that seat staring through the large windows at a clear, cold, blue, winter sky with fluffy snowflakes, seeming to come from nowhere, drifting down. *Grade five?*

Nature's little parachutes
Falling to the ground
Nature's little parachutes
Making ne're a sound.

It was all Moe could remember from the lost poem. Perhaps not a poem worth remembering, but it was his first.

My desire to write seems to have deep roots. No one noticed that and gave encouragement or direction. Back then, my handicap, what's now called A.D.D., kept me ignorant of it. Perhaps I would have taken English grammar more seriously, and Mrs Mackenzie would not have threatened to strap me for my poor spelling.

He struggled through the dense growth down to the creek where the old trail had taken him from home to school each day. Time had erased the path.

Moe looked to where his house had been. Attending school had become such an ordeal that he would look out his bedroom window on cold winter days, hoping that no smoke came from the school furnace chimney. That would mean no classes.

The school and ice rink in winter from my bedroom in 1958
The jet from the perpetually running fire hose for ice-flooding and
building what we called the "iceberg" is in front of the boards.

In spring, when he was smaller, the crust on the snow
supported his weight. When he grew older and more
substantial, it would not. He remembered, maybe in grades
seven or eight, trying it and mourning the loss.

We all wanted to grow up, Moe lamented, *but we soon
learned that adulthood comes with a price. It's good we
only understand that later.*

No trail, no house, no school, no chimney.

He guessed right. The company had spent the
minimum on the fence. It ended hidden in the trees. The
little floodplain showed signs of recent fast, high water.

*Of course, they would stop the fence before here. That
flood would have ripped it away.*

Moe stepped over the creek at the end of the fence.
The open, weedy far side grabbed at his legs as he laboured
back, finally reaching the road inside the gate.

In Copper Cliff, the security guard looked up from her
book. There was no one in view.

Oh well, she sighed, laying the story down. *A chance to try the controls.*

The camera control panel was on her screen, and she clicked the mouse on the pan control. She saw nothing along the fence to the rock face or the opposite way to the trees. She tilted up and panned once more. A maroon car sat at the edge of the scrub about 30 meters from the gate, but *no man, damn.*

The camera would not swivel beyond the fence. The next cameras were on the ring-bus near the river and on the corner of No. 2 power plant and watched the bridge and around to the roll door and the nearby switchyard. Neither was controllable. She searched all the cameras.

Moe searched for another memory. It had been October, not September, when he had stood near here on the low road, staring at the sky after the Soviets had launched Sputnik 1. His mind had been full of awe and wonder. It had seemed that the first science-fiction story he had read, "Rip Foster: Assignment in Space", had come true. His mind wandered forward three more years to the evening Gillis McLennan had planted the seeds of his still enduring interest in the sky, space flight and big rockets. It must have been the summer of 1960, just before Moe took his first scary and wonderful steps away from the cocoon of High Falls and into high school and the greater world. He and the usual gang of kids had been playing some pursuit game or hide and seek, and Moe had run through Gillis' backyard. His neighbour stood in the gathering dark, staring at the eastern sky.

"What are you doing?" Moe asked.

"They put an enormous balloon into space," Gillis said, "Echo I and I'm waiting to see it reflecting the sun. They are bouncing radio waves off it for communication."

It hooked Moe, and he lingered, forgetting the game. Gillis pointed out brighter stars visible in the darkening sky. Gillis lent him an introductory book, "The Golden Book of Astronomy". That Christmas, Mom and Dad had given him a telescope as a gift. That telescope still lingered, dusty, in the little utility shed back home. Moe smiled.

John and I used to lie in dad's big wooden wheelbarrow, covering ourselves with that old, smelly, heavy tarp and look at the stars in the crystal sky. We always thought we saw them move, or other things. Neither of us understood anything of what we were looking at, until I opened Gillis' Golden Book, my door into the universe.

That night in Gillis' back yard now seemed to be the end of childhood and the beginning of his struggle to adulthood. Something, a hidden learning disability Moe now believed had prevented him from paralleling the story of Homer Hickam in that excellent movie, "October Sky". Like Hickam, Sputnik had lifted Moe out of the cosiness of the company town and into a vast, frightening and beautiful universe of the mind.

I launched a rocket, thought Moe, *fuelled by handmade gunpowder. The best shot only rose four feet above the ash pile. Dad watched that success and laughed in startled surprise. I had defied gravity for a brief trip.*

Chapter Three

Moe shuffled along the road towards the power plants. Perhaps he should explore where the house and his father's lush vegetable garden had been. He looked towards the river, beyond the places where Harold Wiseman and Grandpa's two woodsheds had stood. Concrete and steel destroyed the fertile soil that supported Dad's cornrows and currant bushes. Moe wanted to leave it to later, but his heart drew him towards the river, to the spot where an ugly chain-link fence enclosed the site of the house. He expected to find more anger and heartache; instead, the lurking humanity in industrial workers surprised him.

That's the tree! Moe's heart leapt, and for the first time since he had passed the gate, he smiled. As Moe drew nearer, he could see small red fruit dangling in the September sun. The tree survived, struggling just against the south fence of the line-header yard, distorted and gnarled, but it had survived, *allowed to survive* Moe thought.

He reached up and plucked the closest red apple, perfect and without blemish as if it had been waiting for him. He held it in his hand and remembered scooting around the corner of Dad's shop, plucking an apple and...

Moe took a bite of the fruit. Juices washed his lips; the taste drew more memories.

"Donnie, look out there," Mom pointed to the kitchen window behind the family table. Bright spring sunshine poured through, tinted green by the leaves of the crab-apple tree. "The waxwings are feasting on the flowers."

Donnie watched as perhaps a dozen birds or more devoured the blooms for their sweet nectar. It seemed nature approved of their place.

The apple Moe ate, still on the tree by the fence. The only sign left of our home.

Moe's condemnation of industrialism weakened, at least his harsh judgement of those who laboured for the corporations, some of them, perhaps only the workers but the bosses too, protected this precious tree.

He looked around. The fertile space that Wayne Insley had gardened so well, sharing Dad's joy of the land, now sat beneath a sterile, gravel helipad. Moe's bitterness threatened to return. He did not know that another joyful surprise would soften his cantankerous judgement, one more bit of evidence of humanity still living in High Falls.

Moe explored the riverbank and walked along the broken rock that large trucks had dumped there in 1963, to protect the town from the erosion caused by the log sluice. The rest of the space that mowed lawn had covered now hosted a tangle of poplar, birch, and pine. Nature was happy.

The sight of the demolished log-sluice disappointed Moe. So many memories focused on that bit of concrete.

We used to jump and dive from the throat of the thing into the black depths gouged into the river-bottom clay by the powerful flow of the sluice, Moe remembered, *and off the top side into the wash from No. 1 turbine tailrace. Kelvin and I were in the air, already committed in a joint jump, and looked down to see a big Pike, maybe 15 pounds, sunning right below us. They now put these things into movies, in slow motion, but it's always a shark or some science-fiction monster with jaws open. It was that scary to us, and the first time in my life I experienced being aware of my total powerlessness to change an outcome as we hit the water. Of course, we just scared the crap out of that poor fish, but for a fraction of a second, we experienced the fear of doom.* Moe smiled.

His efforts to work up to the road before the bridge took him to his other restorative discovery. He skirted around the swampy ground in the gully below where the cottage house had stood, past an ugly box that served as an office and up the hill. A familiar stone's shape sat on the rock outcrop that guarded the north side of the power plant access.

It's the memory stone! Sudden, fierce excitement gripped Moe. *They moved it and saved it!*

Moe had thought about this stone on the drive into the place. He knew from the satellite pictures that construction had totally disrupted the spot the stone originally occupied, at the west end of No. 2 dam. He had feared they had simply thrown the rock aside. Now it sat in a place of honour, a monument to memory that went back through Moe's embracing the rock to 1907 when a faceless mason had carved his signature onto his work in building Moe's place of remembrance.

I wish I could have met that mason, Moe touched the warm surface, *and I wish I could embrace the men who valued the humanity of High Falls enough to give this stone a place of honour. There are still many good people connected to High Falls.*

I wonder if Tullio built those solid dry-stone walls, especially here at No. 2 tailrace.

The memory rock, carved in 1907 by the mason, Tullio Pellecrini with a tribute to an E. Dionne who might have been a workmate. Gary Moulton, a schoolmate and INCO employee had been responsible for saving the stone.
Photo 2018

Moe quietly walked on past the place he had visited hundreds of times as a child, now become special. He stopped on the crumpled stone above the frog pond. The broken rock slope still angled down into the gully of pussy willow scrub, but a conduit now and a switch stand or some other bit of apparatus intruded into the space the old capacitor stand had occupied. It did not have the softness of the way the jumble of broken rock had filled the spot or the tarred practicality of the old switch platform. It was sterile, industrial.

Children scrambled from rock to boulder along the little ponds and brooks that trickled in the bottom of the deep gorge. Randomly, as young ones usually played, they explored the bulrushes and slimy rocks beneath the water for frogs and crabs. It was September, with a cooling breeze falling through the gorge, and most of the creatures were already seeking their winter mud homes. The sun warmed the rock, and the deep canyon protected everything from the wind.

"Hey, Donnie," Brian called, "I found a frog." The larger boy tried to grab the creature, but it plopped into deeper water and disappeared in the reeds. Donnie arrived, too late. Ronnie came along from the slab of granite on the edge of the rock-bass pond where he had been watching a sunning fish. He was two years younger than the others were but kept pace. They climbed the table rock above the bottom pond and gingerly worked down the crevice to the flat granite finger that channelled the flow east before allowing it to trickle into the last pool. Sometimes, in summer, they went bare-footed here and could feel the rock. Centuries of weather and rushing water had raised lines of harder rock that would feel funny on their feet. The surface looked like wood grain. Now, in September, runners covered Donnie's feet. The trickle of water gurgled over the small falls. No frogs gazed at them from the edges the way they would in the summer heat.

Donnie worked along the eastern edge of the pool, looking for frogs, carefully setting his runners on the smooth surface that sloped precipitously into the water. The far side formed a vertical cliff about five feet high. The dark rock glistened in the sunshine, and wind-whipped rivulets sparkled from the pond's surface.

Donnie felt a strange sensation as if someone were watching. He stood and looked up the steep slope of broken rock and saw an old man who looked like he dreamed with his eyes open, but friendly and somehow familiar.

"I'll be back soon," Donnie shouted to the others who were working their way back upstream. "I have to go."

Moe startled from his reverie. Children played at the frog pond, just as Moe and his friends had done so long ago. He glanced around, no cars, no houses, *where have they come from?*

One kid looked up at Moe as if the boy had been expecting him. The lad laboured carefully through the scrub pussy willows between the broken rock and a solid granite ledge.

Still afraid of snakes, Moe remembered always watching lest he step on or near some harmless garter or fox snake. The women of the town had taught them to hate snakes, actually to fear nature. No one learned to differentiate between a milk snake and the Massasauga rattler that did not live in the valley. Maybe it was just the women's way of trying to make sure the kids played safely. Moe had learned the lesson well, even if that had not been the mothers' intentions, and had struggled for a lifetime to unlearn that silliness.

The boy scrambled up the broken stones, sending small shards rattling to the bottom. Moe remembered that sound from the many times he had climbed this very slope.

The flat stone shards tinkled like broken glass.

"I'm Donnie," the youngster made his way around the newly constructed transformer pen. He seemed self-assured and showed no fear of this stranger. A young Moe would have been more cautious. Donnie acted as if he already knew Moe. The boy had dark brown hair, cut to a brush and an innocent smile that fit his age, but his eyes startled Moe; they did not blink and expressed a mysterious depth that no youngster should possess, as if he had decades of learning and wisdom.

Donnie seems familiar.

"I'm Moe. I see you and your friends are having fun."

Moe and Donnie turned towards the ponds below. The friends had disappeared, and all was silent. He and Donnie were alone.

Gone up to the Rock-Bass Pond, Moe thought in explanation.

That other, bigger pond, just upstream filled the hollow at the bottom of seven-meter vertical cliffs where, before the dams, water had poured over the drop and scoured deep. Moe remembered the hard climb up the notch in the rock beside the pond where they often went up to the higher level. Moe gazed up to the hill beside the powerhouse. It would have been a struggle with the old natural path he remembered, but the new construction made it impossible. He wished he could take that familiar route past the "bottomless pond" towards the fore bay.

He sighed, *if I could only return as a ten-year-old.*

Donnie sat the six-quart wooden basket carefully into a flat crevice near the big depression in the rock. Sphagnum and bushes bearing succulent blueberries filled the hollow, with a few plants of the prized black variety scattered here and there.

Donnie especially loved the taste of the black ones, but he would not today. Berry picking was his first genuine attempt at earning money. He took the old lard-tin with the heavy wire handle and undid his belt, running it through the looping handle and re-buckling. Years later, he would remember those pails. Dad made the containers, and they used them for blueberries on the hills, raspberries, and currants in the garden. At thirteen years old, he never thought about it and worked enthusiastically. People paid good money, maybe $3.00 for a full six-quart basket. Mom was his marketing manager, selling to her friends in Espanola. When the berries were plentiful, like today, it was as good a rate as his father made in the power plants. Donnie set to work, expertly stripping the lush fruit and dropping handful after handful into the tin. He was good at it.

Along with his brother and sister, Donnie had been on the blueberry hills every summer since he could remember. Family times of picking, picnicking and playing on the old tree stumps, burnt out and weathered from the years of logging and forest fires. The afternoon sun warmed him as Donnie dreamt of spaceships and war heroes to break the repetitive tedium of the work.

"I pick blueberries there," Donnie said as if reading Moe's mind. "It's a nice, safe place, and I sit on the top of the rock, look over the big pipe and see the other plant. I sell them at a good price, three dollars for six quarts."

Moe smiled. If you were lucky, three bucks could get you 200 grams now, and the less tasty farmed berries at that. He had picked berries in the years just before he turned sixteen and landed a real summer job at the Espanola paper mill.

Moe had sat in that spot, resting his hands on the weathered granite, roughened even more with splotches of dry, grey-green lichen and saw the view that Donnie described, but Moe thought the trees probably had now grown thick and one could not see past the dark blue penstock that carried water from the fore bay to No. 5 turbine.

The dam above the penstock ran to the west about 200 meters, restraining the water and below, towards the big ponds, dripping water and exfoliated concrete made for an exciting playground. Moe had played there many times.

"We had fun walking to the dam near the big pond. It was fun to play below that dam too, but the company filled it with gravel, and it became boring."

Donnie frowned. "Sometimes I think I'm playing there again, before, you know, they wrecked it."

Moe knew.

However, we were older when they did it, he thought, *and the place had already lost its appeal.*

The security guard glanced at her screen. She had left the camera pointed at the car. It was still there.

There are lots of places he could go other than past the fence.

Then she noticed a flashing LED on her panel. It was the motion detector with the security camera on High Falls No. 2.

Damned broken enunciator, she thought.

She switched the monitor. The high definition camera gave her a panoramic view from the bridge to the new switch stand and line header.

There he is; she frowned. *Damned trespasser, he seems to talk to himself.*

She called her boss.

"Who's on the road?" He frowned at the screen.

"Warwick," she read from the roster. "He already checked High Falls and may be over at the Vermillion now."

"Send him to round up the old coot. Warn him the guy looks harmless but might be demented."

The supervisor watched as the man gesticulated and seemed to talk to the ground and then reached out as if grasping the air.

She punched up Steve Warwick's cell number.

Chapter Four

Donnie took Moe's hand. The boy's fingers felt small grasping two of Moe's. They walked away from old No. 2, down the roadbed that had once carried railway tracks to the big swing-doors. In his youth, this had been a place of grass, weeds, wild strawberries and two wheel-tracks drawn through to the building's doors. Now they had covered it with gravel with only the odd plantain, dust-covered, struggling through the looser parts.

The lightning arrester stand and line header were gone, obsolete technology, but the little concrete wall still filled the space between the roadway and a granite outcrop. The dam dated from 1904, before they tamed the second falls to construct No. 2. The little dam had puzzled a young Moe since no water ever came close. Later, he saw a picture of the awesome power of that wild flow and understood.

The High Falls power plant site in 1907 No. 1 has two generators installed, but they have not yet completed the dam for the canal. The water is rushing through where the frog pond and No. 2 plant are now. Even by the 1950s, the clear-cut areas had lots of trees. This photo is from a postcard dated 1907. It may have mailed to Arthur Philemon Coleman, a geologist who researched the Sudbury area, or he may have taken this photo. Check the Sudbury Library archives for interesting leads.

Taming the river's power had allowed his life here, an earlier version of industrial destruction.

I lament what I have lost, this new soulless version of this place. What of someone living here before the railway, dams, before my town? Would some old homesteader, or more likely a native community feel about their place here as I do now, would they lament the industrialization and before that the rapacious clear-cutting by the loggers? Each generation has a legitimate story of place, but what we call progress would not seem like progress to earlier occupiers of the land.

The thought unsettled Moe. His deep spiritual connection to High Falls only existed as a link in the march of time; replacing an earlier story. The new location of the rock monument confirmed the flow of history through this special place.

Moe had seen the river railing against the leash, in '51 and 1960, and he knew it only waited for men to fail. Even with all of this wondrous, modern construction of concrete and steel, the river waited. It had been here for thousands of years. Moe had explored a possible near future for the Spanish River and the High Falls site in two works of speculative fiction.

Moe turned to see where the water might have gone before the little dam, near where Grandpa's house once stood on the sandbar that became the town-site, and it likely swept through where the cottage that he first lived in had stood just down the hill.

Donnie found the walking hard. There was not much snow, but ice. It had been one of those cold, dry winters, but he was not even two and what did he know? They struggled on, he and his brother, alone, not with Mom, labouring, behind the long building, to where?

The journey seemed an unending ordeal, all black and white like a photograph. There was a hollow and then a slight uphill. That is where it happened. Donnie fell. He wiggled on the ice; the slippery surface and toddler legs would not let him stand. Eventually someone took his hand. Was it his brother? The memory was uncertain. They struggled on, to Grandma and Grandpa's house, over there, misty through cold-teared eyes. The ordeal confused and frightened Donnie but worth it for the comfort of Grandpa's lap.

It was the earliest memory Moe could recall. Many times, he had questioned that memory. Children were not supposed to have memories from when they were so young.

"Grandpa went away. I don't know why. He never even said goodbye." Donnie choked the words out. Once again, he seemed to be inside Moe's head. Both remained silent for a moment, feeling a two-year-old's unfathomable loss.

Grandpa's house on the left foreground
Ours is on the right and the clubhouse between. The view is before 1948,
and likely 1920s before the road as the streets have no tire tracks. The place of
Moe's first memory is on this side of the clubhouse.

*Mom was born, and Grandpa died in that house.
Grandpa went away leaving a big hollow,* Moe thought.

*Maybe, I can't remember. It was all feelings, from the
back of my mind but never to the surface where I could
wrestle with it. I only remember that hard walk, such an
early memory. Maybe Grandpa's arms filled the void from
having to share Mother's arms with an equally deserving,
and now I think displaced brother, but filling an unsatisfied
need, ripped larger by Grandpa disappearing in 1948.
They couldn't explain to a two-year-old what happened.
"Grandpa has gone away. He went to Heaven." Those
were meaningless and long forgotten words. Maybe they
had said nothing. Two-year-olds didn't need an
explanation, after all.*

Moe stared over the hostile industrial site that had once
been the hamlet.

*I heard none of Grandpa's stories of what it was like
when he came here in 1912.*

"Let's climb that cliff," Donnie suddenly exclaimed,
his eyes bright with joy and bringing Moe back to his

present version of reality. "It's easy. There's wintergreen at the top, tastes good."

Donnie scrambled to the rock face and climbed the two meters to the flat top. He carefully searched out the hand and toe-holds in the fractures. The rock was grey and warm. Gingerly, a foot rose to the next grip, sometimes slipping on the first try. Donnie was never afraid of climbing this little cliff. The bigger ones scared him. Brian was already up there, and Beth followed behind.

"I can't do that," Moe shouted his frustration from the roadway.

"Walk around and meet me on the road, past those cedar trees." Donnie carried on.

Moe remembered his caution but satisfaction when he climbed there as a little boy, looking for good footholds on the three-meter rock-face.

He laboured along the high road to the bottom of the steep, road hill, Big Eddy Hill, and began the laborious climb. The asphalt surface was smooth, but age held him in its relentless grip.

Moe struggled higher. The surface of the hill was once gravel that would roll beneath a boy's foot and make him stumble.

A scraped knee, Moe tried to remember.

Once, someone had splashed surplus concrete onto the surface. Vehicles had spun their tires here on the way up. A novice driver might not have carried enough speed into the hill and have to back down and try again. Those were usually weekend fishermen from Sudbury, not used to driving on steep gravel hills. In winter, it had been almost impossible. INCO paved the thing with asphalt before Moe had grown and moved away. It then became the only place in town where kids might even think of braving the slope to roller skate.

We were much deprived, Moe smiled at the irony.

The asphalt came with winter salt, but by then the need for a toboggan run had disappeared, replaced by the greater thrill of Tom Harley's hill.

The toboggan sped down the steep, narrow track of Tom's hill. It was heavy with Warren, Barbara and her mother. Mrs Scott often joined the youngsters in some bit of fun. The sledges had packed a hard icy ridge in the centre of the one lane. If a toboggan slid a bit off, it risked going out of control and heading for the trees. This wild run suffered the fate. The flying beast slew sideways and in self-defence Barb and her mom bailed out, their bodies skidding after the fast-moving craft until they rolled to a stop in the softer snow. Warren, probably lacking time, remained on the toboggan as it headed in a direct path to the trees. In the darkness, it was hard to see what happened, but in a tremendous cloud of powdered snow and ominous sounds, the toboggan came to a rest against the trunks of an ironwood copse. Warren had disappeared. A frantic charge to the little grove found Warren, upside down, with his bum and legs resting against one trunk and his upper body the other. No one could ever say why the crash had not killed him. Laughter and jokes broke the tension. We dragged the toboggan uphill for another run.

Moe reached the first level, gasping for breath. The split rock on the up-slope was still there, but new tree growth had softened and hid the cliff drop towards the town. He made his way on up to the place where the path came from the wintergreen patch at the top of the little cliff. He watched Donnie coming through the cedars that had grown larger now, but he remembered the cool soft spot on dead cedar leaves in those trees where Moe and his friends had sometimes lingered, a cozy secret place on the rock's edge. The other children with Donnie melted into the trees.

"That was fun." Donnie handed Moe a sprig of the mint, still dark and delicious in September. Moe could taste that pleasant memory. Somehow, eating something that had grown on its own was special, tying Moe to the natural world, borrowing a secret from the long stretch of time.

"Thank you, Donnie."

Moe sighed, contemplating the last bit of the hill. His leg required a slow climb. The company had cut back the lip, reducing the slope and making it more manageable. At the top lay another old railway bed built to take the material to the dam construction site way back in 1918.

Chapter Five

Steve Warwick strolled across the Wabageshik Dam back to his truck. He did the weekend inspections of all the power plant sites. The warm fall weather encouraged him to take his time. The phone ringing in his pocket did not bother him. It was not his wife, only someone from Copper Cliff. He would call back, maybe. Two canoeists lifted a red fibreglass touring canoe from the water, preparing to carry it down the hill to the Vermillion River below the powerhouse.

"If you wait a minute, I'll give you a ride in the pickup," Steve called and increased his pace. He enjoyed meeting the occasional travellers, and this was a favourite quick trip for adventurers from Sudbury. The rarer ones on the Spanish at High Falls were serious paddlers, who took the challenging long route from the railway at Biscotasing, maybe as far down as the North Channel near Spanish. Steve backed the truck to the slope down to the river and sat, comfortably above the tailrace on the Vermillion in a little shady spot for his morning break. He let the phone sound several more times and waved at the departing paddlers as he hit the call button. The security guard had finally enticed Steve Warwick to answer his cell phone.

"Where have you been?" The guard demanded.

Steve resented the tone as if the rent-a-cop was his boss. He had never met her. This chick might be hot, but she sounded like the girl who bullied him in grade 3.

"On my break, sweetheart," Steve smiled at the cell. "We unionized guys get them, you know."

He had to rub it in. The security people had lower pay and powerless to unionize. He would have felt sorry for them if they did not make up for it by trying to be high and mighty.

"For half an hour, lucky you," she hissed. "There's some old coot at High Falls, inside the fence. Please," she exaggerated the word, "escort him off. He seems harmless, but he's talking to himself. At least, his lips and arms are moving." Her smirk came through on the phone.

"Damn, I just left High Falls. Okay, I'll get right on it."

Steve hit the red button and put the cell away. He sat to finish his coffee and sandwich.

No hurry, if I wait long enough the geezer will be gone.

The road passed above the frog pond, and in the morning's stillness, Moe could hear the trickle of water through the gorge that had been his joyful playground. He paused, and Donnie took his hand once more. The thick stands of trees screened the spot, but he felt it. Donnie squeezed his fingers. He looked down through the cedars and birch. One cold winter day, when he was older and had a good camera, he photographed a deer at the bottom. It had watched him with big calm eyes. There was another pair of whitetails across the gorge by the penstock at the same time. The deer loved the shelter of the valley in winter, with cedar to browse and some exposed leavings of vegetation.

A deer resting in the snow near the frog pond at -15 F, 1969

"I don't have a camera," Donnie said, "but I want one."

"Take lots of pictures," Moe said, "especially of everything ordinary. When you're my age, the memories won't be ordinary."

INCO had upgraded the road to handle bigger trucks. The green-hat streetlights that had hung from old, weathered poles were gone, no longer needed. There was no one to walk this road at night the way Moe's father and countless ones before him had done at shift change. The need for those men had evaporated. Sensors had replaced their eyes, digital circuits their brains and servomotors, their hands.

"I sometimes walk this road with Dad, at night," Donnie said. "It seems scary, but I am with Dad."

Moe remembered, he had done it only once in the dark, but often remembered that evening walk home with his Dad, 11 PM, after he had spent the afternoon shift with his father in the Big Eddy power plant. He smiled, remembering the bitter-tasting tea Dad had made. It had probably been excellent tea, but there was neither sugar nor milk, and Moe had snuck outside to dump his mug.

Dad was too smart, thought Moe. *He knew I did it and teased me.*

The thought was bitter sweet. The tea taste would come to mind making him feel he had somehow let Father down. He had that feeling many times growing up, but those eight hours had been some of the best times he had spent with his father; that, fishing and picking blueberries, especially the time on the island, near the falls when they had christened the north slope of the gorge "hide-and-go-seek" hill.

Dad and Moe had been picking higher up the hill in a nice damp nook of berry plants and sphagnum moss, when a neighbour came along, lower down doing their picking. Moe thought it had been Mrs Wiseman and one of her daughters. Dad had him lay down beside him, out of sight until the other pair had passed. Henceforth, it was Hide-and-go-seek Hill. Strangely, it had been a bonding moment.

Maybe I got my shyness from Dad. Moe mused. *I never understood why Dad didn't want them to see us.*

"What do you see about the road, Donnie?" Moe gazed on towards the first little rock cut with its enormous cliff on the up-slope side and the toothy stub towards the gorge.

"They removed the big logs, but they're here sometimes."

"You read my mind. Those old red cedar boom logs became too old, and they used them to line the side as a safety barrier. The ugly cable is new." Moe said.

"I only walk beside the logs," Donnie replied. Moe could still see the logs in his mind.

They reached the first cut with its cliff on the hillside, and Moe struggled up a few steps on the jagged rock on the south side of the road.

The view was open here, and Moe looked over the gorge to where the rock shelf, as broad as a roadway, passed along the south side. Brilliant red sumac and golden birch and aspen softened the harsh fracture-lines of the rock. The bedrock ended where, in the early days, workers had built a rock-filled roadbed that travelled past the bottomless pond and up the hill, the original Big Eddy road. Moe never knew if that rock ledge of dark, rust-smudged granite that formed an almost perfect path either natural or blasted out, but the surface was smooth as if worn by centuries of silt-laden water. It also had the wood grain finish like the bottom rock of the gorge.

Goes back to the end of the ice-age, Moe thought, and then remembered the summer that a big slab of rock, maybe 20 or 30 tonnes had fallen off the side of the ledge into the rock-bass pond. It gave him his first lesson that the world always changed. Before that event, he had believed nothing would change. A thought encouraged by the soothing certainty of a small boy growing up beside the always-constant Spanish River.

Moe returned to reality. Donnie had remained quiet and patient while Moe's memories flowed.

"It's scary," said Donnie, "whenever I am on the old flat fishing rock I look up wondering if another's going to crush me."

"The best chance is in spring," Moe said, with the authority of years, "when the winter ice has wedged it away from the cliff. It made me nervous too."

They walked on past the spring in the deep hollow towards the hill where the log drivers used to take a drink and passed through the second big cut. The north face was almost vertical, but the south side leaned over towards the road. When they built the rail line, they had blasted out rock along the natural fractures with no interest in spending any extra effort squaring the thing up. Not like today when diesel fuel for drills and lots of dynamite allowed squared off rock cuts. Just past this big cut, the old road joined the new. There were signs of recent use.

"I guess the maintenance crews go there occasionally. Let's walk down."

A cap of newer gravel covered the way with plant growth struggling through, crushed by the tires of the occasional vehicle. Two rock hills towered ten metres high on each side and framed a natural passage in the hard, grey granite with seams where blueberry plants struggled, now dressed in autumn yellow.

A bird sprang from the rock high above. A big raven, spooked by something swooped downwind towards the ponds, black against the sky.

Nothing seemed to scare those suckers, Moe thought. *I wonder what's up there.*

Moe paused about halfway down to where the road came out above the big pond and looked up to the rocky rim. Nothing was visible. He remembered frightened birds meant a predator somewhere. He wondered but ignored the warning as he searched the gravel road for signs of another old memory.

Somewhere here was the other little spring, between the tire tracks and covered with a wooden hatch. There was no sign of the spring, only weed-covered gravel.

Maybe that wet spot, Moe stared.

The new road now ran across the back-fill of the dam all the way to No. 2 bulkhead.

Logical, Moe thought, *you can do wonders with powerful diesel engines, a luxury they didn't have in 1906.* It looked like they had made many changes to the head-gate house.

Donnie tried the latch on the bulkhead door. Someone had locked it for a change. Often it was open. The black-painted corrugated iron cladding was impenetrable, as was the steel lattice covered window.

"We have to go down and around," Brian said.

The little gaggle of kids scrambled back to where the concrete dam anchored into the rock, slipped between the railing's two-by-fours and into the birch-shaded slope that led to the east. They scampered down to the bottom of the dam and then skirted around the corner of the foundation.

"Watch the muck," Donnie's shoe tried to come off in the soft saturated bog that half-buried the penstock beneath the dam. They scrambled in their wet shoes over the half round of the big pipe.

"What's that smell?" One girl gagged.

"Remember the dead beaver last week in the whirlpool up there," Brian nodded to the top of the dam. "They must have fished it out and thrown it down here."

"That's disgusting," exclaimed Beth.

The odour of decaying flesh saturated and would stick with Donnie right to lunch time.

They gingerly picked their way past the rotting, bloated carcass with the flies buzzing around it and gladly scampered up the steep slope to the steps from the dam to the top of the sun-chart hill. Here black pipes formed the railing. The smoothness felt satisfying in Donnie's grip.

Behind the protecting railing, they watched the whirlpool swirl in the rushing water sucked into the intake. No. 5 generator on full power gulped a lot of water.

At the upstream end of the wing dam that channelled water to the No. 1 and 2 intakes, Moe found a rock to sit on. New construction had caused much disruption. Tullio had carved his monument rock here, the one that now lay in its place of honour beside the road to No. 1 with precise designs of a block wall and levels and squares carved into it by the stonemason when they had built the dam. Only fifty years had passed from Tullio's time to when Moe had been a child, but to him the markings were an ancient mystery, glyphs from the priests of a lost civilization. The stone had become one of his childhood's sacred objects, his pyramids of Egypt.

Chapter Six

"**Y**ou still remember it," said Donnie. "I can still find the rock, sometimes."

"It's down by the No. 1 road," Moe wondered, "haven't you seen it there?"

"I never saw it there before today," Donnie frowned.

"See that old concrete house?" Donnie tugged at Moe's sleeve.

Moe looked up, fearing that the structure would not be there, demolished like the old log chute, but it still stood with its weathered rickety wooden steps and creaking, unlocked door. The poured concrete seemed to be more yellow than it had been in his youth.

Probably too much money to tear it down, Moe was cynical and suffered from the constant sense of loss of the familiar in this childhood playground. It seemed every touchstone was gone or altered. The moving of the memory stone from beside the water rushing to the turbine intakes, as much of a reassuring honour as that was, still seemed like an assault on the preciousness of his memories.

Tullio's handiwork will always be here for me.

"I'm always scared going in there." Donnie stood and walked to the building. The steps seemed as stable as when Moe used to climb them.

"They told me this was where they operated the Johnson valves in the dam's bottom," Moe recalled but remained seated. It was fine for the vigorous young Donnie to explore, but the old man was content with looking.

"Yes, someone told me that too, not sure who. There's a hole in the floor that goes down to the water."

The fore bay from the top of the island
Moe and Donnie sat on the rock in the lower right, and the concrete house is just at the upper edge of that rock. The pine tree hides the overflow.

"I now think it operated something over on the other side." Moe looked over the water to the overflow dam. New construction had removed the old log sluice and left one big overflow right to the rising granite of the far shore. He frowned. A logger had died way back before the dams existed when they sent big pine saw logs down in the spring flood. His grave had been below the old wing, but water now flowed over the spot. He could not see the concrete cross that someone had erected to mark the grave. The work gang had repaired it when he was a kid.

I hope they at least cared about that and moved it.

Moe then remembered that they had moved the marker while he stilled lived in High Falls. They said they moved the grave, but Moe's cynicism thought it had only been the concrete cross. No one would have wanted to touch the bones of the long-dead riverman. He could not see it on the hill beyond the dam.

Water fell over the dam, a lot of water.

"They're wasting water," Moe frowned. In his day, the company tried to balance the flow from Big Eddy power plant with what High Falls could handle. If they put through more than that, they called it "wasting water". Dad recorded the waste on the operator log sheets. He filled them out hour by hour, on every shift after he had finally become an operator in No. 1.

"In my day, the company used all the power in the mines. I heard they sell it to the province now for profit. The more they generate, the more they make."

"They sometimes run wide open," Donnie said as Moe remembered, "at least if it is a wet time. I understood none of that. We play below that dam, down through the big falls and the rapids, but we have to be careful. We even go to the top of the overflow dam and run back and forth on the curved surface. It's kind of scary."

"Yes," Moe recalled, "it nearly caught my buddy Kelvin and me below the falls one day when they suddenly sent more water down."

"Happened to us more than once," Donnie replied.

Kelvin and Donnie moved cautiously along the little bubbling flow below the falls. It seemed much larger from this angle, and the wet sheen of the water falling glistened in the late morning sun.

"It's deep in there," Kelvin said. "Do you see any fish?"

The boys did not consider that it would be unlikely fish would remain in the water-filled hollow below the falls. Every time water poured down it would flush the place out, and fish could not come up the little stream at low water. The cliff opposite the falls loomed menacingly over them. It was already in deep shadow, and a little pine that clung to life at the top cast its shadow against the wet rock.

Slowly, the boys worked back to the rocks where the side channel would flow when more water came over. They struggled to extract a jack-pine pulp log the water had jammed between boulders. They wanted to measure the depth of one pothole in the rock. These were mysterious. *What force could make these holes in the hard rock?* Donnie wondered.

Potholes at the falls, pulpwood logs on the rock
There were bigger holes than these.

Kelvin suddenly raised his head and looked at the surrounding water.

"It's coming harder," he sounded nervous.

Donnie looked up to the lip of the falls.

"I think we need to get out of here." He scrambled downstream looking for the place to climb up. Kelvin followed. Already the water sounded louder, and he could see a surge downstream.

"Quick," he shouted.

The boys scurried up the slope as the water tumbled behind them.

Water in the falls side channel above where Donnie and Kelvin were playing

"That was close," Kelvin frowned, but both boys diluted their fear with the sense of bravery, satisfied they had faced danger and overcame. Below them, the water roared in the channel, not much really but enough to kill. Playing on the falls had the danger of never knowing when power plant operations would dump excess water down the overflow. The boys sat in silence on the hard grey rock, absorbing the scene and the warm morning sun.

Moe looked at Donnie, sceptical. Surprised on the falls had only happened once, and he and his friends were smart enough to learn the lesson. Most of the time the old falls and gorge had a small stream in it or a roaring rush that no one dared get near.

The falls from below
Kelvin and Donnie would have been near where the slash of sunlight is crossing the flow. This photo shows more water than we saw that day.

The small group of youngsters clambered along the grey rock. Behind them, the gush of water falling over the thirty-foot drop churned deeply into the pool before it found its way downhill. A light mist rose. Below them, the little gorge, a river side-channel cut the island in two with the water in flood. It churned and leapt in a frenzy heading towards the lower river. It was spring, not a high flood season, but one of the smaller episodes. It had been a dry winter and little rain in April.

The children searched for a way across, wanting desperately to see the real falls with lots of water. Beyond the rock hill and the big white pines on the far side, they could hear the tantalizing roar of the distant falls.

"I guess we can't," one girl said.

"Maybe we can wade over at the beach," John sounded doubtful and stared at the rushing torrent below. They picked their way carefully. Mist from the falls made the rocks slippery. Donnie stopped and stared down. The rushing water was mesmerizing, beckoning. He shook his head. Donnie remembered the attraction standing on the catwalk above the flume in High Falls No. 1 dam, almost drawing him into jumping in. It was a deadly temptation he always resisted.

"Look there," Brian shouted. Donnie snapped from his reverie.

"We can cross that dead tree." Brian scampered down to where the top of an old, dead cedar had fallen and wedged into the north side of the gorge. The roots had pulled up on the opposite side, but they looked firmly attached to the crevice in the rock that had once fed the living tree. The deadfall made a perfect bridge.

"We can hang onto those branches."

"It looks slippery. I don't think we can," Warren hung back as the group crowded around Brian. He was a bit of a leader, but Donnie shared Warren's caution. Brian had led them into more than one scary adventure.

"I'll go first," Brian usually led by example, and with that, he was onto the tree and heading over. "One at a time," he called. Brian was heavier than most of the kids. If he did not make the tree collapse, they deemed it safe.

One after the other the children took the scary steps. Donnie wanted to hang back. This adventure could get him killed, but the girls had gone. He would not be a sissy. The water threatened, churning white and swift below, beckoning, wanting to embrace him and rattle him through the notch where the enormous boulder nearly blocked the channel, but soon he was beneath the big white pines and breathing again. Once more, he had slain the dragon.

The group took the simple route up to the top of the big hill above the falls. They made their way down one of the big U shaped grooves, ice-carved scratches four meters deep in the granite to a rumbling, misty fury as water, more than they had ever seen roared down the gorge. Donnie's heart swelled with pride. He felt brave, and the incredible sight was his reward. Everyone felt the same pleasure of overcoming fear.

From the top of hide-and-go-seek hill
About where we were looking at the falls the day we crossed the tree.
This photo shows less water than what we saw.

What a gang, Donnie felt relieved when he finally crossed the tree to the home side of the watery gorge.

"You probably have never seen big water going over the falls," Moe went on. "Once a bunch of us, I guess in spring went over there to look. That little gorge, that only has water in it at flood was rolling pretty well and blocked us from getting there. We were brave, or stupid, or both, but there was a fallen dead tree over that torrent, and we used it as a bridge. The falls were impressive and scary. I had never heard them roaring from that close, only a big rumble we could hear from town when there was a flood. We were lucky no one got drowned, stupid now."

"That tree's still there," Donnie said. "We go over it a lot."

Moe gave Donnie another sceptical look. "That tree should have rotted long ago," he said. "Yours must be a new one."

"It has always been there," Donnie mused.

Moe trembled slightly at the memory of that danger, youthful bravery, and his mind moved on to the comfort of the damp, cool, hidden places behind the swimming hole near the scene of their foolishness. In the bush's shade, an enormous boulder sat detached from the cliff. *Maybe dropped by the ice ten thousand years ago,* Moe wondered. *We never could climb that thing, too big; we needed a ladder.*

The shadowy, damp passage compelled. Donnie walked gingerly between the enormous boulder and the vertical wall of bedrock. Both dwarfed him, and yet seemed to offer safety. Even in the summer heat, the place embraced a cool mustiness. His feet sank gently into a bed of leaves, small twigs and some sphagnum. Stunted cedars persisted in damp cracks, while birch, ironwood and hazel shrubs hid the spot. Donnie rubbed a hand on the boulder's surface. Fracture angles made the stone surface different from the smoothness of the big, ice-dragged erratics. The ice had to have dropped it here, but Donnie could just as easily imagine it rolling down from the hill, another mystery in memory full of youthful unknowns.

"Let's get a ladder," Warren looked up to the top that hid beyond the curving surface.

"It'd be too heavy," Donnie sighed. In the 1950s there were no aluminium ladders. "We couldn't get it past the powerhouse."

Defeated once again, they worked their way through the scrub hazel where they often changed into their bathing suits when on a swimming outing, and then past hardwoods to the big pines and the sandy beach.

"We can never climb that rock either," Donnie sat beside Moe once more. "We try lots of times, over and over even doing piggy-back and leaning logs against it, too much moss, wet and the trees too little to hang onto."

"Same as we always found it," Moe sighed. "There'll come a time you won't want to do it anymore."

"I still want to climb it," Donnie raised his voice.

"So do I," said Moe, "so do I."

Mom, Dad and Aunt Beth (Dolby) Prentice
With the famous red rowboat at the swimming-hole beach, the far shore, behind Dad, is where Kelvin and Donnie dug the hole for the shack.

The rocky gorge that had challenged them to cross on the dead tree came out to the river at a little fan made up of smooth, washed stones. It bounded the west end of the sandy beach, the High Falls swimming hole. A big red pine marked the east end of the sand. Moe had learned to swim here, as did three generations of children. It would be nice to sit on that sand again, but the locked power plant blocked the way.

In his youth, there had been a series of wooden stairs and cat-walks over the penstocks behind No. 1. They allowed townspeople get to the swimming hole without going through the power plant. Moe remembered scrambling over it many times. On others, when they were feeling lazy, and perhaps when only the operators were in the plant, they might take the direct route, in the enormous doors, past the generators and out the back door. No one ever yelled at them. Then the log flume challenged them. In the years that the paper company used it to send pine logs past No. 1 dam, the jack pine surging down the concrete channel threw impressive, soaking rooster-tails of spray over the sides. They used to time their dash beneath the flume to avoid getting drenched.

Fun, Moe thought.

He would need to bring a boat up the river and have some fit young people help him.

Only three generations, thought Moe, *Grandpa, Mother and me. The town lived and died so quickly, not even a blink on the eye of history. Even the log sluice is now gone.*

A tear formed.

I won't sit there again, or swim in the rapids or fish there. I wish I could cast that Canadian Wiggler once more.

The rapids when dry

"I do," said Donnie. "I like to sit on that rock near the rapids. There's usually a big pike sunning itself in the water in August. We never can catch it. When there isn't much flow, we swim in the little inlet this end of the rapids. Usually, there's only a trickle of water there, and the big wedge rock in the middle we get to and climb up. We slide down on the smooth rock that runs across the river if there is a bit more water."

Side channel at the rapids with the "wedge rock" where we swam
The swimming hole is just around the corner of the rock on the left.

Moe remembered the rapids rock surface seemed as if someone machined it, but the natural blasting of gravel-laden meltwater as the ice retreated thousands of years before had smoothed it. In his later geology learning, he realized it was the top of a deep dyke of hard rock, perhaps intruded when that asteroid had blasted the Sudbury basin almost two billion years before. It cut across the gorge and tied the hills of the island to the steep south shore. The rapids created many excellent fishing spots. When there was lots of flow, fish gathered in a little bay on the south side. It was good fishing if you could get there when the rapids were roaring.

The rapids are showing high flow.

Chapter Seven

The talk of sitting on rock brought Moe to the present. He suffered from the hardness beneath his bum and stood to stretch. Up the steep rocky hill beside the overflow, on the other side of the intake canal, white pines rose in precarious majesty and then gave way to those big, arrow straight red pines on the crown of the hill. He loved being up there, seeing Big Eddy dam in the sun and lying on the soft bed of fallen pine needles, damp and cool.

"That's my favourite thing to do." Donnie held Moe's hand. "The view of Big Eddy is wonderful. It seems I go there a lot. I explore up on the top, funny, someone carved something into the rock and then wiped it out. I feel old then and sort of remember, but I can't read it sometimes."

"I carved that," Moe smiled at the memory, "when I was older than you and thought I loved a girl before she dumped me. I erased it."

"That's why it always seems familiar." Donnie looked sad as if sharing Moe's thoughts. "I always think I'm not me anymore when I see that."

The boy is too young to care about girls. Life was simple then, and it is for Donnie.

"Girls play with us," Donnie sounded defensive. "They climb the rocks and stuff too."

"See that jumble of big rocks at the bottom of the cliff beneath those white pines nearer the water?" Moe's thoughts strayed from the painful memories of girls. "We would climb through there. It's like little caves. We imagined bear dens and everything. It made it exciting."

"I play there," said Donnie. "I get stung by a big wasp once in a while. Hurts like…" It seemed the little boy could not bring himself to say "hell".

Moe smiled. He did not think he had consciously sworn until university. The first time he had heard his father use "bad language" as Mom called it, was the time Mom and Beth had gone south by bus to visit Grandma in Aurora. Dad had taken Moe and his brother John back into the bush to Denomie's abandoned homestead to get a piece of angle iron from a discarded bed spring.

He brought it back to fix the rotting running board of the old Oldsmobile kept in the big green barn-board garage behind where they built the new school. Dad skinned his knuckles hard with the hammer and swore. It had been so traumatic to Moe's virgin ears that even today, he could not remember the word Dad had used, but he had a good idea. A couple of years later, Moe was not sure how old he was, he had used probably the same word spontaneously when standing with Dad and another man. They had laughed, and Moe had felt humiliated. Trauma still kept him from remembering that word as well. He still cursed sparingly.

Moe had discovered the town had two sides. One part was the polite, Sunday school world where the men did not swear in front of women and children, and the other was the work side where many spoke the rougher language. It was the transition time. Back then, many men, including Moe's dad, always wore a hat and put on a tie to go to town. Saying "hell" or "damn" on radio or television was a strict taboo.

Wasp stings, Moe thought.

As a five-year-old, Donnie thought he was brave, exploring with the others in this swampy ground behind the big green garage. Dad's car was safely inside and the swamp drier in the mid-summer. The children picked their way into the poplar and birch beyond the driveway, towards the hill that led to Brian's house.

"Don't trip on those dead branches," Brian called. Donnie stepped gingerly over a deadfall and planted a foot firmly on a little grassy hummock.

"Eyeeee," Donnie screamed. "Help, oh, eyeeee..." The pain hit Donnie, first in the ankle and then soon his arms, neck and face. The wasps soared from their crushed home and attacked without mercy. Donnie cried as he turned and ran, uncaring for the footing out to the road and made a mad dash for home. The little cohort of children scattered safely into the bush like white-tailed deer spooked by a gunshot.

"Waaah..." Donnie screamed his tears as he rounded the clubhouse and made a dash for the back steps. He had outpaced the last of the angry wasps.

"What's wrong," Mom cried. "Did you break your arm?"

It only took Mom a second to see the rising red welts from the stings. Soon, Donnie stood in his undershorts in the kitchen. The pain eased and soon the dabs of the Dettol, Mom's Plan A for every cut, scrape and bite, added to the stinging; however, it soon had its soothing effect.

"57 stings," Mom told Dad when he arrived home from work. "The swelling and pain are gone now, but Donnie's sore."

"The stings always hurt, the worst I ever feel, except perhaps the day I fall off my bike and hit my arm straight on the ground. I can never throw a ball without that arm hurting now. After that, single stings are nothing." Donnie sounded boastful. He had lived one costly adventure that none of his friends could ever match.

"It was sore after that bike fall," Moe reflected, "but I eventually outgrew it, or it finally healed. We hardly ever went straight down the hill from the red pines to the path that went to the swimming hole." Moe shied away from the memory of that painful sting on his back, or the 57 torturous ones, or Dad's language, so many years before. "I liked to go that way sometimes and see the old log sluice they built years before. It was a concrete trench in the ground, but stopped short as if they didn't bother to make the concrete go downhill and the water washed a huge gully across the path to the beach."

The new log sluice at High Falls No. 1
The upper stub of the original flume goes off at the right. It is the early 1950s as the small penstock that drove the exciter turbines is still in place. The company demolished the small penstock shortly after. They recently demolished the log sluice.

"There's a bridge over the washout," Donnie added, "two pine poles and boards nailed across."

"I guess the one they built when I was young has rotted. Why would there be one now? No one lives here anymore."

"I do, and my friends too. We use the steps and bridge all the time."

"I remember when I was young and there were No steps," Moe frowned. He was becoming convinced that little Donnie was crazy, or autistic or something. None of this could be real now, and the boy had to be only visiting along with his friends.

Where did their parents park? The kid must be making it up to please me.

Moe startled. Somehow, he saw Donnie as important, almost essential. Moe was glad he had met him. It made his visit much better. He had felt lonely, washed in his memories until the young guy had scrambled up the loose rock at the pond and making the shards fly.

He's a shard, thought Moe; *I am too; I splintered off of some old bedrock to play in the sun.*

"Let's get to the dam," Moe began walking back to the main road. "I think it's all different now."

"I want to show you something," Donnie grabbed Moe's hand and drew him away from the road. He led Moe across the gravel expanse that had replaced the shaded rill and its jumble of birch and aspen to the small concrete retaining-dam that joined the rocky outcrop at the end of the wall, to the big rock that blocked their view of the main road. The surface lay damp and moss-covered as it had always been, shaded by mature trees on the riverside.

In the flood of '51, they even sandbagged this little dam. They must have panicked since they didn't bother in '60 and that flood was worse.

"Someone killed a black bear here."

Moe remembered the body of the dead bear lying on the grass in the village. It seemed scruffy and pathetic, helpless. He could not recall who did the shooting.

Chapter Eight

Steve Warwick headed his white company pickup away from the river and up the hill towards the Trans-Canada. He still did not hurry. Usually, on a Sunday, Steve would stop at his house in Whitefish and watch some NFL football before driving to Copper Cliff and booking off. He resented that this intruder had interrupted that routine.

The truck scooted along Highway 17 and then onto Ella Road. This route would take longer to get to Turbine and on to High Falls. Despite missing the ball game, delay suited Steve. He did not want to have to confront anyone, especially what was probably a harmless old man.

Fall colour splashed everywhere. Steve loved his job in summer and fall, winter not so much, and he slowed to savour the beauty. He let the fall fragrance blow through open cab windows, making the most of this diversion.

Why did that old man have to turn up on a Sunday?

"Crack!" something snapped a dry stick among the scrub oaks up the hill.

Movement...oh-oh.

"That's a bear," said Donnie.

57

Too calm, Moe thought.

"Come with me," Donnie clasped Moe's hand and drew him back along the little dam, trying not to slip on the wet moss.

"To the valve house," Donnie exclaimed.

They hurried, Moe wanted to run, but his old body would have let him down, and he likely would never have made it. Behind them, the sounds grew louder, with a snort thrown in to encourage their flight. The bear did not seem to be in a hurry. Moe struggled up the little rock spur and crawled the meter to the top, then down across a slight gully smoother but overgrown with the dead stalks of that shiny grass and stunted sumac. Red drupes of sumac seeds slapped at him as he hurried. That left hip threatened to give out. It seemed the beast followed their scent, to the rickety steps, up, through the doorway. Donnie struggled against the decayed remnants of the door. Moe added his weight and the rusted, dry hinges, protested in one long squeak. Moe thought they might break off. The door seemed too flimsy to stop a mouse.

"I hope the bear didn't hear that," Moe's heart hammered; Donnie looked scared.

"That ought to work," Moe pushed hard against the closed door to divert his fear. It suddenly seemed stronger. *Maybe as strong as when I was a kid but not bear-strong,* Moe frowned.

"Maybe the squeak scared him." Donnie grasped at the hopeful idea.

"The concrete will stop it anyway," Moe trembled. All the old fears and cautions came back. Every time they wandered the bush and hills, they always had an ear for animals, especially bear. There were more bear around now, an excellent result of intelligent hunting and in this place, the demise of the town. Moe had only ever seen one when he was alone and on foot. He had been at the swimming hole, and it was hundreds of meters and a river away, but still a thrill. His heart had raced then.

He had seen the animals from the safety of a car. Once at the High Falls dump, a favourite place for a scavenging bear and the hunters who were too lazy or stupid to track one and give it a fighting chance. Another time, Gillis McLennan had been trying to photograph one from a pile of pine slabs that Chick Dunne had left along the back road. That was the time Moe learned that the idea of actually outrunning a bear would likely end badly. The beast had disappeared in a flash.

This bear was close as if all his fearful imaginings as a child had come to life; however, their pursuer today behaved much more leisurely, not angry or hungry but perhaps curious.

"I've never seen one before," said Donnie. "We ought to be safe. They eat berries, not people."

"That's the theory," Moe tried to smile. "Don't go near that hole in the floor." Moe cautioned. It had always been mysterious and scary. If they had ever fallen into that shaft, they might never get out.

"Shhh!"

Scuffling and sniffing came from outside, the stairs rattled and cracked. Moe peeked through the crack in the doorjamb but could see nothing, more scuffling.

"Sounds like a big puppy, reach out and pet it," Donnie sounded as if he meant it.

"You're a bad influence," Moe chuckled and rubbed Donnie's brush-cut hair.

"Just like you," the boy smirked.

Moe somehow felt relieved to have someone with him. He had usually felt alone when facing a crisis.

Are the sounds going away? Moe wanted to open the door but was cautious.

"He's going down the hill to the big pond," said Donnie. "I wonder where."

"Let me look," Donnie grabbed the door handle before Moe could stop him.

Steve Warwick pulled the truck over and stopped to watch a grouse wandering on the road ahead. It was pecking up grit for digestion. He could hear the bird's peep above the engine noise. It looked like a female chatting away with an unseen partner in the yellowing ferns. Steve was glad he did not have his 16 gauge. He would have shot the bird instead of enjoying it. The grouse disappeared into the roadside brush, and Steve drove off in a cloud of dust and throaty diesel engine chatter, downhill past the little hay field where whitetails often browsed, around the sweeping curve and past the new bungalow towards the bridge on Beaver Lake road. He faced a short drive up the grade to the Regional Road that paralleled the railway line.

The End to My Hunting
I feel the sunlight
warm against
these corroding autumn hills
the leaves brilliant and dying
cooling winds sneaking
amongst the rocks
felling
the corpses of summer
stuffy damp
this decaying deadfall
where I sit
a proud pine before the fire
the gun, twenty gauge but
grown heavy now broken
lying mutely against my perch
laminar trails of smoke
drifting downwind
away to nothingness

from my blasted briar
from below
where the broad basin
half mile square spreads out
rimmed harshly with grey northern granite
the echo drums
upon both my ears
a grouse calling his mate
I have shot

Donnie pulled the protesting door inwards. It had reverted to the almost rotted barrier, and it fell apart in his hands. Big chunks toppled onto him before bouncing with a crash to the floor.

"That option's gone," Moe tried to be light-hearted for the boy's sake. Donnie dusted himself off; Moe stuck his head out the gaping opening. He could not see a bear.

"Good move, Donnie," Moe sounded sarcastic. "You scared him off."

"I always thought," Moe stepped into the sunshine, "that jumble of rocks near the blueberry patch at No. 2 form a good bear's cave. We used to crawl around in there. I remember ice stayed there until almost July. Maybe he's checking out his winter house. It's almost time to hibernate; his food has run out."

"He looked fat," said Donnie.

"We could hardly see it," replied Moe.

"Well, it should have been fat." Donnie insisted.

"Let's go. The bear might not like the doorbell down there," Moe laughed, loudly and nervously, "or he wants a bedtime snack."

Donnie looked up at Moe as if the boy were taking mental notes, his face quizzical.

"What's the matter?" Moe chuckled, "don't you like my joke. Learn not to take life too seriously, take risks."

"I'm scared to take risks most of the time, and I don't like people teasing me," Donnie's face clouded, "or bears chasing me."

"Yeah, it's a hard lesson to learn." Moe's smile faded at the memory of pain.

They hurried back to the road through the rocks and up the grade to the main Big Eddy road. Moe stopped and gasped for breath. It had been years since he had demanded so much from his body. The scare from the bear had pumped more adrenalin into him than he usually endured. The animal was still around, somewhere. More than being glad to distance himself from the bear, Moe happily left the desolate industrial vista of his destroyed childhood playground.

Another one gone, he thought.

The pickup truck eased up the grade towards the Spanish River Road. It used to be old Highway 17 before they built the new Trans-Canada in the 50s. Steve was too young to remember any of that detail. He had known nothing of the Spanish River valley before he took this job. A Sudbury city boy, he had always hunted up towards Gogama.

Steve stopped and looked west. The region did not maintain the road too well in that direction, while more people and company traffic made things better to the east. He eased out onto the crumbling old asphalt.

It would have been better if they left it gravel and just graded the damned thing. It's better than some of those old logging roads I hunt. Steve had the same thought every time he drove this bit on his way to High Falls.

Moe forced himself to walk away from the gap, on towards the dam. The bear would take care of itself. A building of unknown purpose occupied the big flat area on the hillside of the road, backed by trees that went up the slope towards the summit. They had dug dirt, maybe gravel out of there to build the rail line and the dam and powerhouse a hundred years before. It had remained a scrub-filled place when he was young, directly below the blueberry hill, but the trees now obscured the rocky peak.

In the 1960s, Moe had helped build a radio transmitter at the crown of the hill, and a cleared line had run from the road to the summit. They had dismantled it when progress developed better ways of communication over power lines. He saw no sign of the cut in the trees for the line, and in 1995, the last time he had been to the top; the small shack they had built on top for shortwave radio had disappeared without a trace.

Nature claims its own, eventually.

Big Eddy
As seen from the peak of Blueberry Hill in 1968 near where they had
installed the radio transmitter, above where Moe is standing,

Donnie led the way around the gentle curve, past more buildings that had an obscure purpose and towards a jagged rock cut.

"I remember when the log drivers used a bunkhouse here. They tore it down in the 60s after they stopped the pulpwood drive."

"I always hope I can get inside. Maybe the cook has something. He gives me raisin pie at the old camp of tents down by the water." Donnie lingered.

"That was in the 50s," said Moe. "The raisin pie was good. I was a little afraid of those guys. Now I know they were nice."

"Mom worries about strangers," Donnie frowned.

"Yes, my Mom was born here," replied Moe. "She had an aversion to strangers. I caught it a bit, but I am comfortable with people when I get to know them, like those loggers and the work crews."

"I like them. The men on the big truck working on the poles are funny. I think they all have kids too."

A few meters later, Moe froze, overwhelmed by a long-ago feeling. Perhaps the yellow September sunshine had reminded him. One evening, long ago, the whole family had taken a walk up this way, on a gentle August evening, he remembered. Dad, Mom, John and Beth, all had been together. Moe looked at the rock cut, to the tree-covered hill to the north and through the lower bush to where the fore-bay was barely visible.

Here, he thought, *here.*

"Donnie," said Moe, "at this spot, right here, was the happiest moment of my life. The only time I can remember when I felt truly happy and totally safe. The whole family was here. It was as if the evening just wrapped me in happiness."

"I know," said Donnie, "me too."

Moe took Donnie's hand and stood, quietly for a long time. A tear trickled down. Today the sun warmed his back; that August the evening sun had been in their eyes.

How many times in my memory, he wondered, *how many times have I remembered being here in that warm evening and felt healed? How many times in my life when I felt hurt, alone, confused, ignored or lost did this place comfort me?*

Moe looked around once more. The whole place, the warm, safe valley healed him. He could not remember how many times he had stood in this place, in memory. Whatever gale in life attacked him at that moment, he had felt okay.

Chapter Nine

They passed through the rock-cut with its rusty coloured iron oxide traces of the geologic violence that had formed this part of the world. The road branched, one way up to the dam and the other down to the power plant. Moe took the upper route.

Noisy all weather, power transformers sat on the hill above the power plant entrance. The old transformer room would likely be empty now, perhaps with some new-fangled capacitors and switches, but none of the three old transformers it had once housed. These modern machines could handle the paltry thirty megawatts from the plant.

It had all seemed so powerful before. Massive whirring generators, the spinning shafts in the basement, the hum of the transmission equipment. Still, it would take 20 wind turbines to equal them. The wind and water shared a common characteristic; nature decided when the wind blew, or the river ran enough to be reliable. Moe looked again at the steel-grey transformers. They squatted on what had once been a soft grassy spot with an enormous willow tree. He felt the loss of humanness, gentle grassy slopes;

weed-filled borders, toads and snakes replaced with sterile industrial gravel.

Moe remembered cutting grass up here when he was older and had a summer job with the company. The powerful Gravely machine had once hit a hidden tuna tin can and drove it into the trunk of the willow tree. Grass cutting could be as dangerous as the electrical machinery. No tree now, but Moe could still see that can, lodged in the bark, taunting, causing Moe in his youth to think a little deeper about life.

Moe looked back at the enormous door of Big Eddy No. 3.

Dangerous for sure, he thought.

Dad at work at the Big Eddy No. 3 switchboard, about 1958

Dad told that story of being on shift one day when the maintenance gang was cleaning the transformer room. The control board lights suddenly all went red and the generator breakers tripped, just as a blast came from beyond the room's steel doors. Three terrified workers bolted out and did not stop until they were outside. Dad had described Walter looking like a scared jackrabbit as he bolted for the door. Dad tried to figure out what had knocked the whole plant offline. He discovered the men were using a vacuum cleaner, and its cord had touched one of the bus bars. It must have been the low voltage side, since it did not kill them.

"Close but no cigar," had been Walter's attempt at humour. Like everything in life, people answered brushes with death with a laugh.

Walter Edwards, Moe thought, *one of the funniest and nicest men I ever worked with, all those pranks. He scared the heck out of me that time I was inside No. 4 turbine housing, trying to flip open the bottom drain of the downstream wheel well and he hit the outside with a ten-pound hammer, right above my head. He had done the job many times and knew exactly where I was, and that I'd be half-worried that the headgates might fail. Bastard,* Moe smiled and remembered Walter's other pranks.

How many times did I reach for my gloves in my back pocket and have to go looking for where Walter had hidden them? He always left them easy to find. But I got him, Moe almost giggled, *when I made a cottontail from the rag waste we used for cleaning up oil spills and hung it on the back of his bib overalls. He wore it home and to the King George Hotel in Nairn for his usual evening out with his wife. The next day he came into work singing.*

♫Here Comes Peter Cottontail♫

Walter could laugh at himself and taught me the saying that a job was good enough because "a man going by on a galloping horse won't notice". We were re-roofing the long storage hanger for the fire ladders behind the clubhouse.

And the shock on church-going, straight-laced Mom's face when she opened my lunch box after work and the boobs of some Playboy bunny stared up at her. Walter wasn't above putting the mickey to the somewhat privileged residents of High Falls. He always seemed to have a twinkle in his eye.

There were more Walter stories. Maybe Moe would remember them later. Walter's toothy grin and the strange gait when he walked flashed before him.

The little grade rising to the dam was still there, but the rocks towards the penstocks were different. There had been an old hand-held drill bit jammed in the rock, its hole never finished, with a rusty handle sticking sideways welded to the shaft. Moe remembered seeing a movie about Mao's "Great Leap Forward" with three Chinese women, one holding the bit directly with leather gloves but no handle, relying on the other two to swing their ten-pound hammers on target each time. The workers in 1918 were not so trusting as the skilled Chinese women. Today, the drill was missing, another sacred icon from his youth destroyed by progress.

Moe struggled up the little incline and then up the new broad hill road that they had built when they backfilled the east wing of the dam and either tore out or buried the circular stairs. Meters of fill hid the bare dam-face with its concrete sloughing off and pipes dripping water from the inside. He laboured up the slope while the ever-patient Donnie waited a little ahead, beckoning. Finally, he reached the top with a gentle breeze blowing off Agnew Lake. Moe needed another deep swig from his water bottle.

"It's all different now."

Moe looked across the lake, over the bay formed by the half-kilometre dam wall. The bright orange line of a plastic trash boom stretched to the far cliff.

They will soon pull that boom for the winter. We jumped off the far cliff, swimming, Moe remembered, *and we ran that trash boom, red cedar logs, not these plastic canisters, everything's ugly.*

"I run it too, sometimes, when I'm older." Donnie gazed longingly at the lake.

Older, younger, what's the little guy talking about? You can't be both. Time only goes one way, or does it? There's something strange about this kid.

"They put the log boom in all summer after the paper mill stopped driving logs through here." Moe scowled at Donnie. "We were older when they did it."

"They brought the logs down in big rafts. I remember standing on the dam and hearing the tug's diesel engine long before the boat called the KayVee towing a huge raft of logs came around the point making a deep rumble. We would stand on the dam and watch the guys with the pike poles run the logs through the dam. I was young then."

"Me too," said Donnie.

Moe looked down past the dam, beyond the west corner of the powerhouse. He could make out a little of the old log flume, then turned back to the lake and the dam.

He remembered the men pushing logs to the flume entrance, their metal pike-poles flashing in the sun. The bubbling chug of the little "alligator" boat with the front push-rake, as it directed small rafts of logs towards the men. The flat booms were always wet, but the pikers wore hobnailed boots and did not slip, avoiding the current sweeping them along with the timber to a tragic end, 100 feet below in the forebay.

The alligator tug is pushing logs to the pike-men at the Big Eddy log flume.

Pike-men pushing logs into the flume

"A man, not a log driver died on the job. I was young. They were in a boat, trying to get a dead moose carcass to shore. The town's water came from the forebay, and no one wanted rotten moose flavour. A log that came down the sluice went deep and then leapt high out of the water on rebound. The big jack-pine log jumped out of the water and hit one man in the boat. I never really understood until later."

"Everyone is sad," agreed Donnie.

Seeking happier memories, Moe headed down to the water where a dock used to be. A couple of ugly orange boom sections lay to one side. Several families had kept boats on the lake and tied them there in summer.

"We used to try water-skiing off the old dock," Moe relished the scene. "Insleys had a camp over there," he glanced east and could see a building through the trees. "I guess they still do. They had a powerboat and skis, so we all took turns. I got up once, I think."

"Raymond Houlahan went head first off the dock into the water and forgot to let go of the rope. The boat pulled him right out of his swimming trunks. It embarrassed me for him," Moe smiled.

"I always am," said Donnie, drawing another sceptical glance from Moe. Donnie laughed. "I am embarrassed, but Raymond just laughs with the rest of us."

McKays had a camp there too, Moe remembered Harry's smile, *another pleasant image from when the world seemed sane.*

"I took a nice sunset picture from here." Moe once again looked over the water, but from here could see further down the lake. "It was gorgeous."

"I never went into the green boathouse," Moe sighed, "but once I saw it open with a cedar-strip motorboat inside."

"They put it back in the fall," Donnie stared at the spot. "A little dog sits in another boat when it's onshore. Funny little thing."

Moe frowned, trying to remember exactly where the building had been, and he remembered a little brown dog and a cedar-strip runabout motorboat. *Was it Vince's, or Ray Taylor's or... whose..? Who had the friendly little dog?*

Dog on the cedar-strip runabout
The trash boom of red cedar strung in front of the dam

"My memory sucks, sometimes," Moe looked at Donnie.

"Your memories are my life," Donnie replied and scampered provocatively up the slight rise of rock once again to stare at the lake.

They wandered to the end of the dam. It looked completely different, and a roadway ran along the top of the berm where they had backfilled to keep the dam's east wing safe from frost. In his mind, Moe could see the big, concrete end-block. It had said, "1920"; it was the year they finished the dam.

"It was ten more years before the power plant; Big Eddy No. 3 sent power to the mines."

Moe remembered, in the fall of 1969 just before he had gone on his world trip, he had worked on repairing the dam. He pushed many wheelbarrow loads, four bags of Portland concrete mix at a time down a makeshift plank ramp from the top of the keystone block to the mixer on the centre span of the dam.

Prepack Concrete Construction was the contractor Moe thought.

"It sounds like hard work. It isn't for me," Donnie seemed to be in his head once more, "I build shacks," he boasted, "all by myself, but sometimes with Kelvin."

"Let's talk about that later," said Moe.

Moe felt hungry and pulled out a trail bar and the water bottle.

"Want a piece?" Donnie looked scrawny.

"No thanks," the boy said. "I've never seen one of those. I had an Eatmore from Mrs. Insley's store. We collect empty pop bottles along the bottom of the dam. The fishermen, you know, the guys from outside leave them there. After a good weekend, we might have twenty bottles. Mrs. Insley always takes them in trade. The guy on the pop truck pays her for them."

Moe stared at Donnie for several minutes, thinking he saw an apparition. Empty bottles and Mrs. Insley's store were fond memories but long gone.

"I don't think you're real," Moe finally whispered.

"I'm as real as you," Donnie insisted.

Donnie jumped up from where he had been dangling his legs over the edge of the dam's end-block and looked off into the bush.

"We never explored much over there," Moe followed Donnie's gaze away from the lake, into the bush thick with 50 years of extra growth. "I don't know why. It just seemed boring after Blueberry Hill or the island."

"I come through there sometimes," said Donnie. "It's always the same. There weren't too many blueberries. We go up the path to the peak by the cut behind the log-drivers camp rather than go over these rocks."

Moe could not see the bare rock from the end of the dam, but he remembered the scrubby red oak when he was Donnie's age. Once, maybe only once, they had explored from Blueberry Hill to the dam along that ridge. It had been hard going and unfamiliar.

Even the trail up the hill behind the log driver's bunkhouse was a hard steep climb. The Hayward family had climbed it every summer to pick blueberries, but when they were older, without Mom and Dad, the more popular way was to take Tom's road to the first rock outcrop and follow the flatter route over the rocks and get to blueberry peak from the east.

Donnie and Moe retreated down the hill. The grass and shrubs on the fill beside the dam were a contrast to the memory of the bare concrete, dripping drainpipes and the funny cement precipitate that accumulated into hard ripples, slimy to the touch, on the slope of the concrete wall beneath their drip-water.

"Like those rock icicles in caves, I saw in books." Donnie once again seemed to read Moe's mind. "Look at the one with that reddish rusty stain. It's big."

Moe kept on walking. He could see many spots like that in his mind. Somewhere beneath this new backfill, he knew he would find modern drainage tiles dripping water towards the forebay. The buried remains of the winding stairs hid stalactites that formed as the steadily dripping water leeched cement from the concrete. The stairs had been fun, but the company boarded them up after 1960 for safety, and because they put a gate across the east wing to keep the weekend anglers off the dam. No one ever hurt themselves, but by the 1960s lawyers and accountants had more influence in running the company.

The accountants probably spelt the death of the town. Moe clenched a fist in anger. New accounting ideas said that fixed assets like houses were bad for a corporation. Own nothing became the rule.

Moe stared at the dirt back-fill against the dam. In 1920, big concrete dams were relatively new. No one understood the process of water seepage and the impact of deep northern freezes.

Today, if they built this dam at all, it would be dirt and rock stretching from where we swam off the dock to the rock headland where we jumped into the lake as teenagers. The original dam had a particular beauty and thoughtfulness. It now looks like a properly engineered, sterile intrusion.

Moe moved on.

Steve finally turned off the decaying Regional Road onto the High Falls access. He glanced at his watch. He would be at the gate in a few minutes.

There still might be time to get home for a bit.

At the spot where the Hydro One transmission line crossed the Spanish River, Steve pulled over and reached for his binoculars. He walked the few meters to the edge of the high sandbank 20 meters above the river. The far side, in the clear-cut beneath the transmission cables, moose and deer sometimes appeared. Today, no wildlife materialized, with only the odd bee nosing about in the leftover asters and goldenrod at his feet. Steve knew people who hunted in the big bend of the river, but like most land, locals had their hunting territories and strangers usually only went by accident or when invited. Most of the land he saw from the bank was owned by that retired Bill guy.

Good guy, like a one-person conservation movement.

He slid behind the wheel and headed on. Perhaps he would meet a maroon car and could turn around and go home. The game would be in the second quarter by now.

Moe stopped once again where the missing drill bit should have been. Beyond the new frost-wall, he could see the header above the Johnson Valves. It was all different now. The engineers had replaced the black structure for the headgates for the valves with some remote controlled operating gear, like the new spillway system.

Moe's view from near the old drill bit as it was in the 1950s before the new frost-wall and spillway gates appeared near the end of the century. The black gate lifting structure is above the stairs to the Johnson valves just visible going down the face of the dam.

Donnie and the usual gang of kids eased along the dam, past the white bulkhead above the penstocks, over the little steps spanning the log flume and on to the wider area in the centre of the dam. All the stop logs were in the spillways, so it was safe enough. They always made a quick trip to the end of the west wing. They seldom entered the unfamiliar territories of rocks and bush beyond. The children usually played in places that adults had first taken them. Only when older would they venture into unfamiliar territory, and by then the playfulness had faded.

The gang returned to the black mechanism on the dam and looked down the steep stairway to the roof of the valve housing, always a scary challenge. The group went ahead, gingerly descending the steps. Everything was open steel, no kid proofing here. Donnie grasped the lower pipe of the handrail, warm in the bright morning sun, not looking too far down. The gaps in the bars of steel tread created confusion. If you stared through them, you might become dizzy and stumble. The steel structure switched back and then a final steep, straight bit to the roof.

"Try the door," Warren was eager.

The barrier resisted Brian's push, but it reluctantly swung inward. Sometimes, someone locked the door but not today.

They went down the short flight of stairs inside. The windows allowed subdued light. Decades of condensation had yellowed the windowpanes. The spookiness attracted them as much as the challenge of the stairs.

Being good industrial kids, they knew enough not to touch any controls. None of them knew what went on here, and the fearful mystery held them in check. Three big round tubes filled the lower space surrounded by a concrete walkway. It smelled of decaying concrete, rust and mildewed wood. Slimy ripples had formed in the cement where water leaked through the dam. Flakes of concrete littered the floor. It was cool and damp as always and silent. Perhaps the silence threatened the most, only broken by the ominous sound of dripping water that hinted at the enormous pressure behind the base of the dam. The Johnson valves were large butterfly valves designed to drain water and silt from the bottom of the lake. They used the valves at spring flood time. The children did not linger. They had met the challenge once again, and they made the slow, tiring climb to the top of the dam.

Donnie looked at the watch he had worn since Mom and Dad had given him the timepiece in Grade 3.

"Lunchtime," he announced. They scurried off. It was a long walk home.

Moe smiled at the memory. Even though there had been many fears and doubts in his childhood, there were, like the Johnson valves and the dead-tree bridge, many times they had overcome those fears.

Johnson valves house with the steep stairs from the top
The black structure on top is for the valve headgates–photographer
unknown

Donnie gasped as he finally got his foot onto the top of the wall. They had crossed the catwalk over the three penstocks and were now on top of the retaining wall that separated the rear of Big Eddy powerhouse from the flood when they opened the nearest spillways. He peered over. Below was about a two-meter distance to concrete spattered rock below the first spillway. It led along the bottom of the dam, but the descent was formidable. They walked down the 30 meters of the wall to just at the powerhouse and then stepped onto the rock a few centimetres below. There was a problem with this route. The top of the wall was flat but only two feet wide. It sloped away towards the penstocks at a steep angle, and one point on the dam side dropped vertically about six meters. It was a challenge, a demand for bravery to a little boy who made that walk. Still, it would not defeat him. Everyone did it, although Donnie was sure it scared them too.

The retaining wall the kids crossed to get to play below the spillways.
This photo is from the 1930s as there were no covers on the penstocks after I was born.

The spillway side was a foreign land with a few scrub maples that washed away, or stunted when, about every ten years, all the floodgates handled exceptional spring runoffs. It was a typical rocky walk back to the dam on the rough but safe ground. The reward was to go down a few feet and walk on the bottom lip of the spillways right to the wall of the Johnson Valve house. Most of the time they got wet feet because the stop log system leaked.

Some of the Big Eddy spillways from the roof of the Johnson valves
The view we saw as children with the sheen of the water leaking from between
the stop logs.

"Do you think those stop logs will break and kill us?" The thought worried Donnie.

"For sure," said Brian with his weird sense of humour. "We're all dead."

Usually, they did not linger on the lip beside the menacing dark water of the forebay that here seemed to have no bottom.

They boosted the smaller kids up the log leaning against the wall, right at the dam, followed by the biggest kid who did not need help.

"I'm glad we didn't have to walk back that way," Donnie looked down the narrow wall where they had been so brave an hour before.

Spillways wide open washing over where we played
They caused the flood down the river in 1951. We can see why they
needed the wall to protect the power plant–photographer unknown.

"Let's go," Moe took Donnie's hand. "I can't think
about this place much more."

The new vista depressed him. No children would ever
explore here again. He looked at Donnie.

"Yes, I'm usually tired and hungry after playing here."

Moe ambled back towards the town. Despite the
depressing changes, this was a wonderful experience, but
he wanted to linger somewhere he could see rocks, trees
and water and not the changes. The gentle hum from the
power plant faded behind. The sun arched past zenith, but
he wanted to look at more places and remember.

Chapter Ten

Steve guided the truck up from the creek and concrete bridge. He did not know the big house on the corner of Edwards Road was one of the High Falls houses, the biggest one where Bucky Mcquillen had lived. He slid over the hill, past Sutherland's place and down and up the gully, beyond Vince Houlahan's old house and onto the flat where the Whites had farmed. None of these names was familiar to him. He had never stopped along here, and because he was not a day worker at the plants, he heard no gossip or history. Steve did not know that the house on the corner, where a road went to the hydro right-of-way north of Agnew Lake had served as a store and lunch bar, back in the 60s when everyone thought a uranium mine up that road was a sure thing. The mine had come and gone within ten years, perhaps a stock scam or a victim of falling ore prices. Steve had hunted along that road. Gravel berms and a slab of decaying concrete were all that remained of the old mine site. The road now served the Hydro One transmission line.

Agnew Lake Mine head frame 1969

Tom Harley had just about killed himself building a road back to the old Smart homestead eight miles into the bush. He had married Joe Smart's daughter, worked as a floor man in the power plant, and died young, of cancer. Two years later, the mining company built a paved road that passed within 100 meters of the old homestead. Tom's road had probably killed him but became an excellent path for hunting grouse.

The view from Tom's road above Denomie's valley
I composed my poem about quitting hunting while sitting here after
taking this photo.

Steve drove past the equally unknown, long closed old
High Falls dump. It no longer fed any black bear.
Only a mile to go, five minutes he thought, *why hurry.*
Steve frowned; *the old bastard must still be there.*
He slowed even more.

Moe did not linger where the road branched down to
the place they had fled the bear. He knew the animal would
poke around somewhere, but when he reached the toothy
rock cut above the bottomless pond, he stopped. No bear in
sight, he watched a beaver carrying an aspen branch to its
lodge on the opposite side of the large patch of water. The
cutting would be part of the beaver family's winter pantry.
Beaver had used the pond forever, as Moe remembered it.
He recalled that a guy from out of town used to set beaver
traps in winter. Moe resented the trapping then but had not
realized the struggle for survival of people who did not
have well-paying industrial jobs. Moe understood now, but
happy the beaver persisted.

Donnie stepped across the little stream that drained the bottomless pond. A few twigs stripped bare of bark by the beaver had lodged into the channel sides of the brook. He scrambled to the top of the humpy rock outcrop. Donnie could see the line of Big Eddy road high above and the little rock cut. He wanted to reach there, but he would take the route around the pond and over all the fractured rock where they had dumped stone from the cuts to make a stable bed for the railway. It was man-made, but to Donnie, it was part of the natural order in the valley. The angular boulders challenged, and the small fractured bits at the top made for an uncertain climb. He finally stood on the flat road after wiggling over one of the old boom logs guarding the drop. Moe waited for him at the rock cut.

"We played there," Moe stared down the jumbled slope Donnie had just conquered, still light grey after all those years as if only blasted out recently. "We more enjoyed playing in the bush and dam on the far side."

"We do too," Donnie replied as the two stared across the broad valley.

Steve Warwick eased the truck up to the gate. He stared glumly at the maroon sedan that sat defiantly beside the road.

Damn!

The gate was remote controlled, and Steve punched in the code; the barrier slid easily on greased rollers. Steve waved at the camera on the pole to the hillside of the contraption. His phone rang.

"Well, it's about time," the guard sounded cheerful. "I was going to send out a search party for you." Her chuckle was infectious. Steve did not harbour grudges. He did not even know the woman and laughed back.

"If I'm going to get lost, sweetheart, this would be a nice place to do it, with you of course." The beautiful weather and relaxing drive had mellowed him.

"Hey, you're married," she threw some cold water on him, "but what's the offer?" She flirted back.

Briefly, Steve thought over his grievances in his marriage, and then he saw the much more significant list of benefits, family and love.

"Too late, sweetie, but my buddy is available."

"Let me think about it. Keep his number handy. Does he have a job?" The guard smiled through the phone. "Do you see the old guy?"

Steve rolled the truck through the gate.

"No, but I'll find him quick. There aren't too many places to hide from this great hunter."

"Yeah sure, when's the last time you shot a moose, dear?" Her smile sounded through the phone. "Let us know when you get the guy. He looks harmless."

The truck grumbled towards the power plants.

Moe had almost reached the top of the hill when the sound of a vehicle made his heart race.

Not yet, it's too soon, he thought, *I'm not done yet.*

Steve looked up Big Eddy hill but went to the lower plants where the guard had last seen the man.

Maybe he's too old to climb the hill. Steve remained optimistic.

Unknowingly, Moe being old and slow intervened and prevented discovery. A few more meters and Steve would have seen him exposed at the hilltop. Waiting for the little boy had used up a useful minute, although Moe believed the people in the truck would soon discover him.

"Donnie, come with me, hurry, stop dawdling."

Moe turned from the road, struggled through the ditch and onto the tree-filled flat of the old railway bed that passed above the town-site. Thick weeds grabbed his legs and feet, while tree branches formed a living fence, but this tangle protected him, and wrapped him in invisibility.

Another hide-and-go-seek-hill, he smiled, *but any decent hunter will see our tracks.*

It was slow work, and his legs felt leaden. He turned to call for Donnie to hurry.

Where is the boy?

Moe looked around. His heart pounded once more. Donnie might reveal where they were or got himself lost, and Moe would have to go looking for him. When he finally turned to the front, there was Donnie, smiling and holding a branch so it would not slap Moe.

We used to do that in the bush all the time going through single file like now. If someone forgot or wanted to be a smart aleck, someone else took a hit in the face. No one played that trick much. There was no way of being sure anyone would be at the front of the line next time with revenge always possible. Moe took the branch in his hand.

Donnie stayed in front. He never let a branch snap back.

The sound of the truck passing towards the powerhouse reassured him. Moe risked discovery to peer out over the engineered scree slope that had been another support for the trains. The trees were thick here, and he could see Steve Warwick's brake lights flare near the entrance to No. 1.

I should have all afternoon if I stay out of sight.

The flat track-bed had overgrown since Moe's childhood. Then it had been mostly open. They used to find railway spikes amongst the crushed slag, imported from Copper Cliff for track ballast, and the occasional tie plate and other nameless hardware. Moe looked at the changed space with child-like eyes, imagining hideouts, brush forts, and other joys they could have built with this. They had done it often but not here.

"We come up here, through these poplars," Donnie looked at some aspen that grew in a denser patch on the dirt at the east side of the rock fill. Kids climbing here had worn a trail into the hillside.

Mom's generation played here too; Moe had never thought about that before, that his generation had followed in the footsteps of the first gang of kids that grew up in High Falls. *Another bunch followed us, but they were the last.*

Karen Evershed and Terry Insley 1969
Two of the next generation after ours, Terry's Dad and Karen's brother would be familiar with our special places. I have so few photos of this last generation, many of whom were not much younger.

What did that last generation experience? Moe wondered. *Did they find some of our special places? Did they stray down the river to the sandpit, all over the island and explore Big Eddy and the hill? The town had already changed, physically and socially when I left. There were fewer children and more restrictions. They stopped making the ice rink, at least the one we enjoyed.*

Vicky Jo Houlahan and Missy LeBorgne 1969
Two more of the last generation

Moe looked about. He could not see Donnie anywhere. Moe's questions did not interest the kid.

Our generation played in a different place than Mom's group. We never had the rail line and the stress of the depression. That's life, I guess.

Some bigger dead trunks were in various stages of decay, but fresh growth filled in the space. In Moe's childhood, they could stand up here and people in the town not see them. Now, the people in that truck would have little chance of spotting them unless they walked into the trees or went up to the cliff above.

Moe looked at the dark grey wall of rock. The new trees gave it a damp sheen, not the dry grey, moss-covered surface of his youth.

High Falls never really evolved into a village, Moe mused, *because people always left when the man retired; it was still the men who worked in the plants, and many went away because of a promotion or just wanted to live outside the village, in town where social opportunities attracted them. The Mackenzie's were the first I can remember, and Art commuted here to work every day. I'm sure we thought it strange then, but it makes sense now. We saw that urge when we hit high school, and I know my sister felt it much younger than John did or I. As boys, Dad put us into Espanola hockey. For Beth, I never thought of it then; she did not go to things like that.* Moe wandered further.

Summer jobs, Moe paused... *another difference. We boys all got good paying summer jobs with the company. The girls didn't, at least not in our generation. It seemed normal then. Women have taught us a lot since, but I wonder if that has changed. I wonder how many men think about this, even now.*

Many of the young women I met later, the ones from small towns all seemed to express dissatisfaction and even hatred towards those little places. I think women, more than men feel the isolation and limits. It's probably worse for girls growing up than boys, like our experience. The smartest person I ever met, the woman from Listowel in university expressed her ambivalence to her hometown, and she is a thoughtful person. I didn't appreciate her feelings. I never thought I would find some new understanding today, curious...

Moe eased along, picking his way amongst the grown trees until he came to a little rock outcrop from the main cliff. It was rounded and comfortable. A large juniper bush still grew in a little nook. Its blue coloured berries hung between the needles and the place had the slight odour of gin. Instinctively, Moe looked beneath for snakes. He had never seen a snake here, but always thought they might be there. *Maybe the Yankee Western Matinee on television and its rattlesnakes in the sagebrush spooked me.*

Moe sat. Suddenly the morning's effort had caught up to him. Fatigue overwhelmed. He took a long drink from the water bottle and glanced at his watch.

Nap time. Moe closed his eyes. Donnie remained quiet.

Chapter Eleven

Steve Warwick walked around the parking area in front of High Falls No. 1. There were no tracks in the dust, other than the tires and boots from Friday's work gang. Still, it did not convince him, and Steve climbed the first set of stairs for the catwalk over No. 4 penstock. No sign of anyone, and looking up the three-meter pipes he could see no one at the dam.

Donnie expertly climbed down the vertical wooden ladder from the catwalk in front of No. 1 bulkhead to the plank landing on top of No. 3 penstock. He had done this many times. Several friends followed. The tall wooden stacks of the pressure relief system towered beside him to the upper walkway. Below was the risky joy of "running the pipes", as the kids called it, down to the wooden walkway at the bottom. The pipe dropped 60 feet and made the slope a challenge. Cold water flowing inside the penstock created a slippery coating of condensation on the outside. They were playful but not crazy, and everyone was cautious. The only time there had been an accident, Brian

Insley slipped off No. 5 penstock into the gap between the pipe and the cut rock. There were no broken bones, but he needed some therapy for a few months. It made them all, especially Donnie, even more cautious, but it did not stop the game despite new parental rules.

Donnie picked his way down No. 3, avoiding the access cover with its many bolts, stepping gingerly over a line that marked what he would later learn was an expansion joint and finally to the safety of the lower, wooden catwalk, familiar and safe, the way they took most times to the swimming hole.

It was more fun coming down this way than by the steps. That climb involved a steep combination of flat stones cemented to form steps and a wooden stairway over a near-vertical drop half-way up. This morning, Donnie had stopped to watch a porcupine scale an aspen tree, seeking safety from the rowdy children. Higher up, by the second set of stone steps, he had picked blueberries.

They had climbed on a quest to the little building where they kept the sun chart. From the top of the flat-roofed shack that looked like a glorified telephone box, the entire village spread out through the trees, and the long line of the mountain towered above. The little building had served as a police guard box, protecting the officers on duty at the dam. Dad worked here as a cop at the start of World War 2, before he went into the power plants.

Mom and Dad, Maurice and Betty (Prentice) Hayward
In his INCO police uniform in 1942 on the rock path between No. 1 and
2 bulkheads, with the police box, sun-chart hidden behind them.

A platform with a wooden railing held a mechanism for measuring the strength of the sun. A sizeable, perfect, glass ball magnified sunlight onto a ribbon of special cardboard, coloured blue and marked out in hours. It burnt a strip of varying size that recorded the strength and duration of the sun and the amount of cloudiness. Long ones were for the extended summer days and shorter ones for winter. Part of the careful weather monitoring had taken place at High Falls for decades. Each day, the floor man climbed to the chart house and changed the strip, bringing the day's chart, carefully dated back to the plant. At the morning shift change, the plant operator would stop at a Stevenson Screen at the east end of the tailrace bridge to record the temperatures and the maximum and minimum. Weather monitoring would be one casualty of the conversion of the plant to remote control and eliminating the operating jobs. Donnie was ignorant of it all as he scurried down the steps to the parking lot and headed home for lunch.

They told a story about those penstocks; Moe's memory went beyond that fun activity of the running, stairs and sun chart. *Grandpa Albert, during World War One, had succumbed to his mischievous side. As Dad did in the second war, police guarded the complex against potential saboteurs working for the Kaiser.* Moe smiled at the silliness, but he had learned how propaganda could stir up fears and hatred. *One cop was a sergeant with a handle-barred moustache, someone full of himself. There had been the roof on the penstocks then and Grandpa, working as a floor man on the afternoon shift had gone up to the dam. He had taken a large wooden barrel and rolled it down the penstock cover. When it reached the bottom, it had built up speed and exploded against the back wall of the plant with the staves flying everywhere. The self-important sergeant came rushing out waving his double-barrelled shotgun in all directions.*

The cop could have killed Grandpa, and then I wouldn't exist, Moe frowned and chuckled.

Steve Warwick went back down the catwalk stairs and tried the door to the office area and pump room, then around to the big equipment door.

They had moulded the words, "Huronian Power Co." into the long concrete capstone to the doorway. Steve pondered. *There's a history here. Maybe I should learn about it.*

Steve had not been a brilliant scholar, but that was due more to boredom than lack of intelligence. His favourite

TV shows, other than sports were all about hunting, nature and history. His children already showed interest. Looking at the capstone, Steve thought perhaps local history might be fascinating. It took a half-hour to check all the little buildings and doors, and the entrance to No. 2.

Steve talked into his cell as he looked up the formidable stairs that went from the powerhouse to the bulkheads. He had called the security office.

"Could that old coot been fit enough to climb these steep stairs?"

"How should I know?" the guard responded. "I've never been there and don't know what you're talking about."

"Many people say that," Steve smiled. "My buddy Pierre oversees some work here. Why don't you ask him to give you a tour? Do you like fishing?"

Matchmaking suddenly seemed part of Warwick's job description.

"Okay, what's his number?" The sigh was audible. "I rarely like blind dates, especially when my source is a blind smart ass who can't find an old man. I only know you as a voice. You might be fat and ugly and your friend too."

"The blind leading the blind, sweetie, I might be ugly, but Pierre isn't. If you two hit it off, Deb and I'll have you both to dinner, and you can see what you missed out on."

"I don't go for girls," she laughed.

Steve gave Pierre's number and punched off.

The truck eased across the bridge over No. 2 tailrace and headed for Big Eddy hill.

Resting on the rock, a hundred meters and impenetrable forest of trees from where the road reached the flat upper way, Moe closed his eyes and drifted in memory. He could hear Donnie laughing. He looked to where the little boy had been. Donnie was away, scrambling up the rock face at a place Moe had often attempted. An old memory, an old fear came to Moe.

"Watch out; you will fall."

"Oh," Donnie gasped, several meters above the old track bed and slid back down, the toes of his worn sneakers grabbing enough to slow him, his hands clutching at bits of moss and lichen. He came to rest with a thump on the old rail bed and examined his sore, dirt-covered hands.

"Wow! That was fun. I do that often, at least a few times. I never know when, but I would need to be up there. Once I made it all the way, but mostly I slide down like that. I always have to try. My brother climbs it easy."

"Won't your parents be worried about you?" Moe had seen no other car at the gate.

"Oh, Mom never worries. She knows I'll be home when it's time, or she'll blow a whistle if supper is ready."

"Where's home, Donnie," Moe had a brief thought of the long gone white, green-roofed house where he had lived.

"That's where I live," said Donnie, "in the big house." "I play here in the town a lot." Donnie smiled.

"But there is no town." It puzzled Moe.

"There isn't because you are looking at it now. Close your eyes and I can play some more."

"I always felt all alone and small; and it seemed I was always short and afraid of getting hurt, even when I got bigger." Moe drifted far away.

"I do too," said Donnie, jerking the old man back to reality.

Moe looked at the boy, and suddenly Donnie seemed smaller and fragile.

"I only ever won one fight," said Moe.

After school, the day Donnie had beaten Ronnie in the schoolyard and torn his shirt right up the back, Donnie waited nervously in his backyard. There was a gap between the coal shed and Dad's shop. Donnie peeked through the opening, past the sweet crabapple tree to the street. Ronnie and Brian were walking past, Brian looking tough and Ronnie tentative.

I hope they don't see me. Donnie could not look away even as he risked discovery. *I don't want to fight. I could beat Ronnie again, but Brian would thump me.*

The pair disappeared behind the gigantic tree, and then, peeking around the corner, Donnie saw Brian wait on the street as Ronnie went into the safety of the little house beside the river. Both Ronnie and Donnie were safe.

"I beat one kid," said Donnie, "but he's the only one. He's the teacher's son in grade six and has to walk past our house on the way home. Brian escorts him home like I'm a threat. I think I'm more scared than he is. I can't remember why we fought. Most kids put me on the ground, even my brother."

"I only thought later how his mother, our teacher never took it out on me. That gave me a lot of respect for her in later life," said Moe. "It sucks being small, or even thinking you are small. I never learned to play any sport in my head until I was much older," Moe added, "maybe because I never learned to live my life in my head, at least then. Even when I got bigger, I always saw myself as small. Somehow, it made me afraid of being physically hurt. Some would have called me a coward."

"Dad coached John and me in hockey, but my brother got all the attention. It frustrated me trying to be as good as him. It made me feel stupid."

"I try so very hard," said Donnie, "but it never seems to be good enough, but I can skate good," he smiled proudly.

"Well, Donnie, the word is well. Learn English; you will wish you had later."

There was a pause.

"I'm still small," Donnie exclaimed.

"Sometimes, I am too," Moe sighed and looked to the west.

A truck roared up the hill. Trees screened Moe's resting place, and he could not see the vehicle that he assumed was the one that had gone to No. 1 powerhouse.

"Whoever that is will find us eventually," Moe frowned.

"Not too soon, I hope," Donnie shook a stone from his sneaker. "I want to play more."

Chapter Twelve

Steve concentrated on the road until he reached the flat. He did not notice the disturbance of the weeds where Moe had led Donnie into the bush. Steve knew nothing about the railway that used to run here and that there was even a bit of flat track bed running 100 meters east. The truck hurried on, raising dust, with the roar of its diesel getting lost across the valley. Steve still hoped that he would easily find the man either along the roadway or near the lake.

Steve sped past the turn to the fore-bay dam and now in a hurry, rushed towards Big Eddy. He followed the upper road to the dam. It was apparent the man was not on the lower way, and Steve pulled over by the transformers and walked down to check the powerhouse.

I should have rushed right over; Steve thought as he slid behind the wheel after a fruitless search of the plant. They locked everything tight, and he saw no footprints other than his own from the morning inspection. He sped up the hill to the lake. The time now seemed to be significant.

"Grandma," said Donnie, "when is the show on; when can we listen to Maggie Muggins?"

Grandma Prentice pointed at the wall clock. "See," she said, "right there it says fifteen minutes to three. At three o'clock the show comes on, and we will listen."

"It's my favourite," said Donnie, "about kids and they have fun, but I don't know what that clock says."

Donnie pointed to the clock on the wall. Grandma disappeared and returned with the alarm clock from the bedroom and set it on the blue-checked oilcloth covering the kitchen table.

"I'll teach you to tell time. Sit here in the chair and look at the clock."

Donnie was eager. He climbed onto the white wooden chair with the high back and stared at the clock. He knew the numbers, but did not understand what they meant.

"The big hand tells you the minute, and the little hand tells you hours. See, now the big hand is at the ten, and the little hand is almost at three. It means it is almost three o'clock and time for the radio."

Donnie stared. "But how?" he asked.

"The big numbers are hours, and the little marks are minutes." Grandma seemed smart. "Count the little marks between the big hand and the twelve." Grandma pushed the clock closer to Donnie. He counted, pointing his finger at each mark.

"Nine," he said.

"So it's nine minutes before the hour, and look at the little hand. It's about to point at the three, three o'clock, and so the clock is telling you, it is nine minutes to three."

"Eight, now," exclaimed Donnie, "it's only eight."

"Because the hand is moving all the time," said Grandma. "When it is at the twelve, the little hand will be at the three."

"What makes it move, Grandma?"

"Little springs and gears and do-dads," Grandma smiled.

Donnie watched as the big hand crept to the top of the dial.

"It's at the top," cried Donnie, "It's at the twelve."

Grandma and Donnie went to the living room. The big green eye flared bright, and the radio crackled to life, sending out the familiar music, and then the beautiful voice of Maggie Muggins.

"Where are the hands now, Donnie?" Maggie Muggins had said goodbye, and Donnie was happy. He loved that radio programme. Maggie was a friend. He looked at the clock.

"The big hand is at the six, and the little one is halfway between three and four."

"Count the marks from twelve to where the big hand is."

Donnie counted. "Thirty!"

"The little hand is halfway from three to four," Grandma smiled her kind smile. "How many minutes is that?"

"Thirty," cried Donnie.

Grandma explained how the clock worked. By supper time, Donnie could read the clock. Days later, he had perfected it. He loved his Grandma.

Moe had received his first watch on his next birthday.

The cottage we lived in until 1954 before we moved into the big house.

"That was my first house," said Moe. "Mom and Dad and John lived in the little cabin beside Insley's house but moved to the white cottage before I was born."

"Mom says the little cabin got its water from Insley's garden hose," Donnie added.

"It was hard there, after John was born, from what Mom said. She was glad to move to the white cottage."

"Mom says there was once a black bear on the roof of that cabin." Donnie laughed.

Donnie and Moe shuddered together, remembering their bear just a few hours ago. They glanced nervously through the trees where a bear could lurk, unseen.

"There was never a bear near the cottage, but lots of skunks." Moe smiled, remembering the family of skunks that lived in the big steel drainpipe that came from under the high road. It was right in their sandpit play spot. He relived the pleasant memories of trucks, highways and sticks and stones miniature houses the kids built there.

"All the kids, especially Bucky, come there to play. The sand feels so nice and warm in the summer," said Donnie. "We can't take the wooden trucks that Dad made outside. They bought me the farm tractor and then the yellow grader. John has the yellow dump truck. They are great in the sand."

Dad made me the red semi-truck for Christmas and a dump truck for John in 1951; the grader was a later present before 1954.

Moe squinted to Donnie, doubting every word, but they were all true. It was many years ago, in the past.

"I remember the year Dad made the wooden trucks," Moe warmed at the memory. "He built his lathe to make the wheels and hand-carved the cabs. One day, in November I think, we went outside, and Dad was in the red shop behind the house with the door open. I saw one of the truck cabs sitting on his bench. He hadn't painted it yet. We surprised Dad, and he shut the door. The next time I saw that cab, he had painted it red and placed it under the tree on Christmas morning." Moe's sigh was huge and full of love. "I can see so clearly that unpainted wooden sculpture, shining white in the dark of the shed."

The memories, even the hard ones now sweetened by time roiled in his mind as the water did at the bottom of the falls, with big splashes of time suddenly leaping into view.

When they washed against the hard surface of reality, they left a bright sheen, a memory of their passing.

"We would sit in the dark living room on winter nights, Saturdays, and listen to Foster Hewitt call the Leaf games." Darkness, warmth, and togetherness with his barely visible father and brother suddenly surrounded Moe. "Dad loved the Leafs. I think he had dreams of playing. Dad played hockey well, but a fatherless kid from Kettleby had no chance." The big green eye of the Deforest-Crossley shone as Ted Kennedy scored another goal and Foster's loud cry of, "He shoots, he scores!" filled the room. "We couldn't help but be bit by the hockey bug in Dad's house."

Moe paused, exploring the warmth of that happy memory. The difference in age and ability amongst the Hayward males did not matter in that darkened room washed in the virtual glory of the beloved blue and white. Moe could not remember when his sister, Beth had cheered for the Montreal Canadiens, to be stubborn and put the mickey to her brothers.

"They've only won the damned cup three times in my lifetime," Moe almost snarled, "all three in the sixties."

"They haven't won it yet," Donnie replied.

Moe looked at the little boy, *innocent kid.*

"I don't care anymore," Moe was suddenly angry. "It isn't the game of Armstrong, Bower, Horton or Shack, just a bunch of overpaid entertainers playing too many games with no emotion. They only try hard in the playoffs, playing in June for money on soft ice in places ice is not supposed to be, in front of ignorant fans who never even skated but only want victory and blood. Hockey is supposed to be over in April."

Moe breathed hard and slumped harder onto his stone perch.

"Calm down," Donnie seemed to talk to himself. "It's only a game. I want to do something fun. Think of something fun."

Steve did not stay long above the dam. He saw a set of new footprints that seemed to make a random path. He looked into the trees, towards the camps, but the tracks did not go in that direction. They seemed to concentrate at the end of the dam and then from there, head back down the hill.

I must have passed him, somewhere; Steve sent the vehicle down the hill.

Maybe he's at No. 2 dam.

Moe's mind returned to the present. Everywhere he looked, the river, the empty town site, the power plants peeked through the trees.

So many places, so many good times, a gap in the trees let him see the end of No. 1 plant and the door into the office and pump room, that housed the shower.

"Come on, kids, let's go have a shower." Mom stood at the door of the cottage with an armful of towels. John, Donnie and Beth already had their bathing suits on. Showers made for a fun time. There was no shower in the house, just the old claw-foot bathtub. The cottage did not have a hot water tank, but a water-heating jacket in the firebox of the kitchen cook stove. In winter, it was available all the time, although they had to be frugal. In the summer heat, Mom tried not to have the stove lit too much. The shower was a break from that heat.

The little Hayward procession went up the hill and over the bridge in the gentle late August evening. Donnie always felt the excursion was to a place of mystery and a little scary.

"Touch nothing," Mom always reminded them as they passed through the brick-arched doorway and into the pump room.

"Stay away from that oil," she said, sounding like she was talking from experience. "It won't wash off."

They reached the shower beyond a noisy motor and opposite the big tanks of thick oil that operated the hydraulics in the plant. Donnie stood, fascinated every time by the giant golden brass piston lifters that would slowly rise like mysterious sea creatures, oil soaked and gleaming in the incandescent light, and slowly dive beneath the dark brown surface. These old pumps, installed before Grandpa had first worked in the plant in 1912, still faithfully pressurized the pipes. Their large piston pumps let them run at a slow speed. The pressure was low, and the noisy motor on the other side ran a high-speed centrifugal pump delivering higher pressure to somewhere. The shower door, opposite one tank, led to a little dressing area and the curtained shower stall beside it.

They showered in their bathing suits. Mom was not comfortable with nudity, although Donnie remembered that when they were younger, it was okay. He dropped the soap onto the slippery wooden duckboards that covered the shower floor. The slimy wood disgusted him, but the water was warm and soothing and a real adventure. Mom's hands massaged the shampoo into his brush-cut hair and scalp. He sighed in pleasure, but the stinging eyes from the soap followed. Once again, he had not remembered to keep his eyes closed.

With everything but feet dried, he slipped on his warm pyjamas, shy at his nakedness, then out to the entrance room near the office to sit on a toolbox, drying their feet for socks and shoes

They passed out, beneath the green-hat light reflector with its big incandescent bulb above the door. Moths flitted in the light, noisily hitting the lamp and the white metal surface. Bug shadows played on the concrete doorstep. Even in the summer heat, their damp bodies always felt the coolness. In northern places like High Falls, daytime temperatures seldom lingered long into the evening.

They made their way home through the night with the stars peeking above the yard lights, past the steel stairs to No. 2 entrance with its green-hat door light. The whoosh of No. 2 tailrace in the darkness below the bridge seemed ominous. Donnie, feeling it safer walked on the side beside the big wooden box that carried the town's water pipe across the tailrace. They filled it with chips and sawdust to keep the water from freezing in the dead of January. In the daylight, Donnie enjoyed crossing the bridge and sometimes, when the kids were alone, they would walk along the broad flat top of the water conduit enjoying the dangerous thrill of being high above the water. If an adult saw them, they would yell at the children. If they fell off, well, that was the thrill, the risk. Donnie thought about that without putting it into fancy words inside his head.

Visits from our cousins were an enjoyable part of growing up
Here Aunt Beth, Carol, and Robert are with our family, about 1952. The transformer pen sits to the right with the bridge over No. 2 tailrace behind to the left with the box cover over the town's water pipes. The door to the powerhouse and the pump room shower is behind the photographer, likely Aunt Ethel.

"We do so many neat things around that bridge," Donnie ran his hand through his hair as if wiping away the last of the shower water.

Moe thought about it all. Beneath the bridge had been a strange, scary and exciting place.

"Be careful near the water," Dad said as he slipped a worm onto the hook on Donnie's fishing pole. The birch stick held a few yards of braided cotton fishing line wound around the end, black against the reddish bark-covered yellow wood. The line tied to a leader with a lead sinker clamped above. Dad handed the pole to Donnie.

"Sit on that rock and don't reach out too far. If you catch one, I'll help."

Dad took his rod, the stainless steel one with the nice Shakespeare reel, and gingerly slid down the slight inclining rock until his feet found solid support on the little ledge. Dad carefully laid his homemade brass gaff hook within easy reach. Donnie could see Dad's white running shoes a few inches from the swirling, dark water of No. 2 tailrace. It was loud and scary with the turbine at full power, but Donnie felt safe with Dad and Mom here. John already had his line in the water and Beth scrambled around behind, exploring the shrubs and boulders. Mom sat contentedly letting her line swirl in the back eddy near the concrete bridge pillar and as usual, complained at the lack of fish. Catching a two-pound pickerel would cheer her up.

Eventually, Donnie grew bored with no fish and joined his sister. The timbers and cross-braces of the bridge provided a challenge and an opportunity to climb. Donnie looked at the steel beams that carried the span over the water and the wooden timbers and railway ties on the east end where points of light flickered between the two plank tire tracks that replaced the original steel railway tracks. Bird nests occupied the bottom flanges on the high beams that rested on massive concrete pillars.

I enjoy coming here, Donnie thought. He looked up to the little patch of blue sky, visible between the bridge and the towering wall of the powerhouse. Red bricks glowed in the afternoon sun.

A dry stone wall about five feet high buttressed the road high above which went to the big service doors. They built it with the plant thirty years before Donnie was born. He tried to climb the wall, but it was vertical and so nicely made that the stones offered little space for his toes.

I know I can do it; he fumed, *but not today.*

Chapter Thirteen

Moe eased a little higher up the smooth rock to find a more comfortable spot. He used the heels of his shoes to push higher. The dead moss covering flaked against his pants.

Mom would not like the stains, thought Moe, *but that's not her problem now.*

Moe gazed through the trees. In the distance, two lines full of clothes fluttered in the breeze and stretched to the two old telephone poles Dad had installed just past the cold frames and at the redcurrant patch. He could almost hear the snapping sound the clothes made on windy days.

Is that Mom hanging the last of the wash from the stoop at the corner of the house?

"Donnie, please get the tub stand and tubs from the shop." Mom pushed the Beatie wringer washer from its resting place behind the chair near the cook stove.

Donnie with Lucky
The wringer washer is in the corner in its cover. Mom celebrated finally getting an automatic washing machine. Dad cut out a section of the kitchen counter to install the washer and made a cupboard out of it. We still have that cupboard in use in our front porch.

Donnie went through the screened porch to the shop and brought the wooden folding tub stand. He knew the routine. Then he put the two big galvanized washtubs used for rinsing on top. Mom poured big buckets of warm water into them, once the hose had filled the washer with hot water. In some strange ritual that Donnie never understood until later, soap, likely powdered Tide or Cheer went into the machine and some other liquid into the first tub leaving clear last rinse water in the second tub.

"Donnie, please sort that pile into whites and darks and put all the underwear into the bleach bucket. We don't want germs."

The washer suddenly went into action making a repetitive thumping and water sound.

"Clunk, clunk, zurp, zurp, whoosh."

Donnie watched the swirling soapy water and the occasional rise of clothes to the surface. Mom aligned the washer and tubs so that the rollers with their little chutes hung over the first tub.

"Okay, time to rinse," Mom turned off the agitator and twisted the knob that sent the white rubber rollers into action.

"Donnie, take this stick and lift the clothes into the roller," Mom would always repeat the instruction, reflecting the rarity when Donnie was there to help.

Donnie used a weathered wooden stick, a grey colour from a long history of washdays, to lift one piece of clothing at a time out of the hot water and direct the cloth into the rollers that squeezed the water out to flow back into the washer as the clothes dropped into the first softener-laced washtub. Once empty, more clothes went to be agitated. Mom, then swung the rollers out, and moved the washtubs, riding on their rolling stand back so that she could wring the clothes out from the first to the second tub.

"Okay, Donnie, use the stick to swirl the clothes in each tub to make sure they are all rinsed." The last wringing operation put the cleaned clothes into a store-bought laundry basket that had replaced a large garden hamper. From there, it was Mom's job to lug them outside and hang them on the line with the wooden spring pins. Donnie always thought of them as little alligators, and it was fun to put them on the end of a finger and be brave. Occasionally she used long, straight wooden pins that reminded Donnie of the Skittle people in a "Noddy" book.

Mom repeated the operation until she completed the week's laundry. Donnie found it boring and only later understood Mom's dedication to the family and the dull routine that it required.

"You can go play now," Mom said at last. Donnie bolted to the door.

Moe remembered lines of flapping clothes everywhere. He was close enough to hear Mrs. Wiseman's wash snapping just below the hill.

"They freeze solid in winter and Mom brings them in from the line and hangs them on the wooden clothes horse. Our long Johns are always like boards for a bit until they melt." Donnie sat beside Moe.

"How come you always know what I'm thinking?"

"Don't you know?" Donnie smirked and slid from his rocky perch.

"Where are you going?" Moe did not feel like moving and stretched his left leg out to ease the discomfort in his hip and knee.

"Up there," Donnie pointed to the worn path that skirted the east end of the cliff above Moe's head. He scampered off with the low shrubs slapping at his legs and disappearing behind the rusty leaves of the hard oaks.

Faye led the little cohort of children as they laboured up the steep hillside. The path, like much of the town and everywhere in the shade held ice and mud late into the spring. Wet dirt acted as grease on the still frozen undersoil. The kids climbed beside the depression, bending low on the steep slope, clutching at the shrubs when necessary but determined to reach their goal. Donnie laboured to keep up, not wanting to show any weakness, especially to Faye who teased him she was older.

They reached the sloping meadow above the cliff, warm and bare in the mid-April sun. Deer browsed here this time of year, but if they were nearby, the noisy children had scared them into the bush-covered flat, higher up.

Donnie looked nervously towards the lip of the hill where the steep drop went down to almost where the railway had been. In the summer, he would have ventured closer, but in the slippery spring thaw, he dared not do it.

The kids went in single file to the smooth rock formation at the west end of the clearing. It looked like a rounded loaf from below, but they trekked towards the broad ledge that ran across the face at the base of the rock. They called the shelf, "the Chesterfield" and sat there many times, laughing, talking or sometimes alone in what passed for kid's deep thinking. The place unified the children at play, and they could look out, past the few tall pines and over the birch trees at the river and town spread below.

Donnie sat. "Do you think Indians ever came here?" He always wondered if Indians had made the trails.

"For sure," someone said and made a mock war whoop, patting the palm of their hand against their open, warbling mouth. Everyone would laugh with no knowledge of real natives. Even though surrounded by several native communities, the town existed in an insulated world.

The place warmed and comforted in the spring sun and worth the struggle. It was still too snowy to venture higher, as they would in full summer.

Moe waited for Donnie to tire of the climb.

The truck eased between the two rock walls towards No. 2 dam. This time, Steve could see the marks on the road that could be foot tracks. He expected to corral the old coot here. The truck stopped near the dam and Steve clambered over the rocks above the dark water. Eddies and bubbles swirled around with the ominous sound of the flow dropping over the flood wall on the far side.

Maybe the guy slipped in here and is dead.

Steve winced at the thought and was hopeful. If he had gone into the water here, it has carried the trespasser down to the generator intakes and not over the drop on the far side. Steve began walking down the dam, searching the fast-flowing canal for any sign of a body or a living man clutching at the shore. His mood had soured.

Chapter Fourteen

"**W**here am I playing next?" Donnie suddenly appeared beside Moe.

"Why don't you go take a hike?" Moe seemed grumpy. Donnie had disturbed a catnap. Moe looked down to where the creek reached the river on the edge of town. He could see the old road that went a bit down river from the back lane. The trail led to the sandpit.

Donnie searched through the pile of rusting cans, other old junk and shrubs beside the little bush road, looking for coloured glass or, if he was lucky, a whole bottle. Beth had once found a beautiful blue glass bottle here. The junk remained from the garbage dump of the construction camp when they had been building the plants and dam. Mom said there were 3000 workers here at the height of the construction but left the dump as the only trace. It had only taken nature thirty years to reclaim most of the old camp.

Disappointed, Donnie hurried on with the gang. They were going to what they called the sandpit at the bend in the river, where the river ran out of sight downstream from High Falls.

Beyond Insley's dock, where the flat-bottomed motorboat moved restlessly on its mooring in the light current, the path had overgrown and another place where it was essential to dodge branches that would slap his face.

A large tree, fallen across the path required scrambling, and then over the little swale where the swamp behind drained into the river. Donnie only learned later that the way followed a low river levee, and the swamp was a standard feature of such places. In playful youth, these were too serious for thought. The ground became easy, and they scrambled down a sand hill to the flat that bordered the river, a moonscape of piles of washed rock, gravel and sand.

The river picked up speed here as it passed through a narrower gap and over a shallow, rocky bottom that resisted erosion. Here would be where Donnie would learn about river navigation. The swift current washed the near shore, but on the far side was a back eddy from the bend and then only slight current if you hugged the far riverbank. In Dad's red rowboat, when he was old enough to go on his own, Donnie would row back from down river along the far side and then cross to the town much higher up where the current would carry the boat to the mooring spot near the foreman's house. Today, the object was fun, not work.

The children climbed slowly up the rock pile beside the "hopper". It was all that remained from the construction, and where they had separated sand from rock to make concrete. They must have done the work by hand, or with horses and the loads taken up the narrow road constructed through the swamp to load on a railway car where the line crossed the roadway. Donnie had seen no sign of how they did it. The hopper, with its wooden-handled levers, steel plated inside slopes, chutes and large piles of rounded stone teased his understanding of this fun place.

They reached the top; the flat stretched away from the river again part levee, but who cared? Donnie stood on top of the lip, looking down at the open sandy slope that reached almost to the rushing water. It was a scary challenge the first time but now was fun. They were about to do in summer what they usually did in deep winter snow. One by one, the kids flung themselves off the lip, hit the sand feet first and then flopped over to roll, laughing to the bottom. Only a few yards of flat stony beach kept them from reaching the swift water.

"You look like a sand-kid," Brian laughed at Donnie. Donnie laughed back. Here it was not an insult. It never occurred to Donnie that Mom would not appreciate the sand in the washing machine. They struggled to the top for more. They would have tried a toboggan here, if it had not been too much work to carry it from home.

Moe looked down the river, past Insley's house to the black spruce and cedar of the swamp. The place interested him, and he lamented he had never become the geomorphologist he had once wanted to be. He could have spent a lifetime researching and documenting the Spanish River valley below the escarpment. Insley's house rested on the back-slope of a considerable hill of broken rock that might have come from the construction, but in those days, it was too far to move it, and there was plenty of blasted rock piled nearer the plants and dams. It was more likely that the river had put it there, thousands of years ago as a spillway for the melting ice. It had a gentle curve that paralleled the river, an unlikely way for construction workers to have left it. One thing he might have spent a lifetime trying to explain, a vast, stone river levee testifying to the ferocity of the 9000 years old glacial melt.

To the north of that, the road ran against the base of a high hill made of clay and sand, with a flat bench at the top, before a little rise to the bottom of the exposed escarpment rock. It looked like an old riverbank and beach made when the water was a hundred meters above where it now flowed. Right at the road sat a deposit of yellow varved clay, with brown organic seasonal layers, a classic formation that he might have devoted a full research paper to explain its place in the ten-thousand years of valley formation.

Moe sighed.

I doubt anyone will bother now. There are too many spectacular and famous landscapes to explain, and grant money would be available for those.

Donnie and Kelvin pulled the little wagon out to the road and up the small hill past the garages. Donnie had Dad's round mouth shovel, and the pair were on a mission.

"We'll take turns digging," Donnie said as he stuck the blade into the hard clay. The township had fixed the ditch here and exposed the yellow earth. Kelvin and Donnie wanted clay for moulding pottery. It would be a half-hearted project, but for now, it was their quest. With Kelvin, Donnie was bossy and did most of the digging. It was his dad's shovel, after all.

In gathering clay, Donnie carved a nice flat surface that had thick layers of yellow separated by thin, brown layers. The boys would be in high school before either of them learned about the rarity of varved clay.

It's looking for a needle in a haystack, Steve mused. He stared into the swirling water at No. 2 intake, watching the deep whirlpool swirl around.

Steve went to the bulkhead door and rattled the latch. The lock was in place, but his master key soon had him through. No one was inside, but he wanted to check No. 1 and the top of the hill, just in case the old man had climbed the steep steps.

Concrete steps took him from the dam to the top of the hill, but he saw no one. No. 1 bulkhead was empty of life, and he did not see a body on the penstocks.

Steve seldom came up here, and paused, leaning on the rusting pipe railing to take in the panorama. The river beyond the plant was serene and dark-blue with windblown rivulets making silvery patches on the surface. Golden birch and aspen dotted the far shore, highlighted by the dark of black spruce. A blue jay scolded him from pines and birches to the southwest. He did not know what this view looked like in the town's heyday. Steve felt peace, as he often did when hunting and taking a quiet moment in the bush.

Steve would have seen this from the catwalk but without the houses
I took this photo in 1968

Steve looked at the rusted steel ladder and the tough jump from the end of the catwalk to the dirt path at the island. No signs betrayed someone's passing, and it was likely too challenging for a frail old man.

Damn, he thought, *I've run out of options. There is too much to search for one guy.*

"How often do you play hide-and-seek, Donnie?" Moe shifted for comfort.

"Green-light 1... 2 ... 3 red-light," Faye's voice rang out from beneath the streetlight. Six children, advancing to her base from thirty yards away froze.

"Green-light 1... 2 ... red-light," Donnie waited eagerly for the next command. He wanted to reach base and be the caller but seldom did. The others were usually too fast for him, but he kept trying. Soon, Faye would tire of teasing them and cry "Run home". They would make a mad dash for the green box that housed the fire hydrant beside the black, steel lamppost.

Ready

One more cycle of red and green and then run like mad.

Donnie was not last this time, he beat his kid sister, and she was fast. Brian would be the caller this time.

"How come you are always the caller?" Donnie asked Faye.

"Because I'm older than you," she said this often. Donnie never took it nicely. It fed his already considerable uncertainty about himself. He never had an answer. He now remembered her with fondness.

They all ran back to the starting line, waiting for Brian to tease them towards the goal.

"Red light isn't „hide and seek', Donnie."

"Ready or not, here I come," Beth's voice rang out from the usual home base beneath the corner streetlight. If a hider touched the pole before the seeker and called "home free" they were safe. The seeker could decide whoever would be the next "it", but by agreement, it was usually the last caught. First caught ended the game too soon.

They played the game any time of the day, but the children preferred dusk when the streetlights were on and cast shadows you could hide in, and the spookiness made it thrilling. Donnie and the others had learned to wear dark clothing for the evening fun, camouflaged like little commandos in training. Unlike larger towns, there was no danger from humans in High Falls, and wild animals stayed clear when humans were about, except for the arrogant skunks. This game was fairer than red light. Donnie often avoided capture.

"Those darn skunks would give humans the finger if they had fingers," Moe laughed. Donnie looked puzzled. In his protected world, he had not yet discovered the "Italian salute". Moe remembered the countless days and evenings whiled away in games.

"Ally-oop-over," John threw the tennis ball high over the clubhouse roof. Six kids waited, poised on the balls of their feet waiting for the team on the other side to come charging around each end of the building. The tactic was for the receiving unit to split into two, and one of them would carry the ball. The throwing team had to run around the building to become the receiving team, but the trick was to avoid the end of the person with the ball. If you chose wrong, the ball carrier would throw it at one of the fleeing kids, and if the ball hit, the victim changed teams. Gradually all the players were on one side and then the game started over. In reality, it was like flipping a coin, and the game could end with no result except for a bunch of tired, and happy children.

"Look out, Ronnie has the ball." Donnie had picked the wrong end. The ball caught him in the ribs. It did not hurt, but there was always the instant feeling of defeat, quickly followed by bonding with his new team.

"I'll throw it," Brian looked at Donnie, "you take too many tries to get it over."

"My arm's strong," Donnie insisted, but usually it took him several tries to get the ball to trickle over the peak. Brian heaved, and the ball soared high over without touching the roof. "You can carry the ball next time," Brian laughed. "You don't throw hard, but straight."

Donnie rocked on his feet, switching his attention from one end of the building to the other.

Where's the ball?

Where's the guy?

Steve wandered back to his truck beside No. 2 bulkhead and called in for help. He now had a lost man somewhere on the property, maybe in the river or lake.

"I'm going off shift," the guard replied. "Are you staying there until they find him?"

"Yes."

"Here's my cell. Call me when you find the old coot but not after midnight," the guard giggled. "My name's Andrea."

"Maybe I should get Pierre to call... after midnight."

"Don't you dare, I'll call Pierre. I want to be in control."

"I'd better warn him," Steve chuckled. "Okay, as soon as I know, or in the morning."

Andrea called her boss. Once his ranting about "stupid old people" ran its course, he dialled the backdoor number to the OPP emergency operations office.

"They're sending a cruiser now with two cops. The call has gone to round up more officers and auxiliaries, but it's Sunday. It will take time."

"The marine unit and divers are just finishing recovering a body in Lake Penage and will be awhile. There isn't much chance of a real search before dark. Let's hope the old beggar shows up."

Chapter Fifteen

With nothing better to do than wait for the cops and more people to help search, Steve returned to the maroon car. It was unlocked, so he slid into the driver's seat. The keys were in the ignition.

Strange, he didn't care about it being here when he got back, if he got back.

A chill ran down Steve's spine thinking that the man might not have intended to return.

He rifled through a pile of papers on the front passenger seat. He found a collection of maps, tourist brochures, a receipt from a motel and a notebook. At the bottom of the little pile, he found a thick photo album. On the front, someone had written the words: "High Falls Memories", in a neat hand using a black marker. Beneath was a dash followed by the word, "Moe".

I guess we are looking for Moe, Steve thought.

Before he opened the album, Steve searched the glove compartment. The registration said Moe lived in southern Ontario. A gate pass said it was M. Hayward.

Steve called the security office. Andrea was gone, and a man's voice answered.

"The guy we're looking for is Moe Hayward," Steve read the pass. "He might have been staying at the Spanish River Motel in Espanola. Maybe the cops can check. He's alone here, but there might be someone there."

Steve rattled off the address in southern Ontario on the car's registration. The OPP would follow that up.

He opened the photo album.

"I took pictures from up here," Moe patted Donnie on the head, "up there at the top of the cliff. August haze was in the air, but everything was green, and lush; Dad in his garden probably; people fishing or cutting grass; the new generation of kids playing where we used to."

"Where I play," Donnie answered.

"Where you play," Moe sighed, now used to the kid's strange comments.

Fascinated by the pictures, already feeling the loss for a place he had never known existed, Steve, opened the notebook.

"I come and feel sad," were the first words. "It would have been better for them to abandon the whole place and return to nature than become this ugly industrial monstrosity desecrating our playground, our home, our place. I have no room for hate, but I see cancer, the cancer of money eating everything."

Steve looked out the car windshield at the fence, slightly rusted grey and beyond to the ugly squat storage buildings and the big ring-bus towards the river. He felt Moe's sadness. *It pays my wages, but...*

He flipped back for a brief look at the first picture in the photo album, of the school in November snow.

And that was when it was already declining, Steve thought.

Steve read on.

"I fought battles on the field between Dad's garden and the creek, a loner kid acting out glorious wars. Sometimes I struggled towards the stream, my imaginary Somme or Rhine River. The school was on the far side, my Passchendaele near where the roads crossed the stream beneath the rocky hill, my Vimy Ridge."

"The first real, comprehensive book I remember reading was a history of World War One, the „Great War.' In a single schoolroom with eight grades to teach and mostly under trained or old teachers, there was lots of time to read. The pathetic little library hid behind the piano at the back of the classroom."

Donnie finished his arithmetic and looked around. Mrs Mackenzie was busy with the grade eights, and his other classmates were in various degrees of struggling with the work or using pencils as rocket ships. Donnie slipped to the back of the room, behind the piano, to the refuge of the books. Here awaited an oddball collection of little readers, kid's storybooks, and un-vetted volumes of who knew what.

Donnie had often read the kids science books, the old volumes of, "The Book of Knowledge", that answered questions like, "why do cement sidewalks have slits cut into them?" Information on frogs and toads, rivers, and other natural things, many were wondrous and familiar in this bush town. He spied the thickest book on the shelves, "The Great War". Donnie could not resist. The 1200 pages of mud, blood and mayhem became his refuge for many weeks. Eventually, his legs tired from standing on the tiled concrete floor with the book open on the linoleum covered counter; he took the thing to his seat. Donnie found it more comfortable at his desk with its light varnished wood, curved backrest and the large steel tube frame. He could ignore the buzz of other lessons, and Mrs. Mackenzie could relish the fact that he was not as restless as some others were. Only when the teacher talked about something interesting, history especially did Donnie wander from the death throes of a maddened world.

Inside SS4B Drury, the High Falls school, in the 1950s

"I disappeared," Steve read, "into the bravery, tenacity and victories in those 1200 schizophrenic pages that went from document and horror to vain-glorious propaganda. My heart beat with the pride of an ignorant colonial boy, relishing our; victories and the smashing of the cruel Hun.

"Still, in those pages were the seeds of understanding of the horror and uselessness of war; 10,000 dead, 60,000 wounded; 2500 dead horses; 220 field guns destroyed; no territory gained after weeks of terror in a battle that in the end had not affected the outcome. Later in life, I came to understand the ugliness of places like the Somme."

"The effect took years to sink in. In Grade 10 in Copper Cliff High School, for a project to use „... ing' words for Mrs Sparling, my English teacher, I wrote a poem about the huge explosive mines tunnelled beneath the enemy trenches and set off as part of an attack, killing hundreds of unsuspecting soldiers."

"I submitted the poem to the yearbook in Grade 11 at Espanola High School and ended up getting interviewed by an English teacher. I think the school was afraid I was suicidal or something. After all, in the 1960s young people were only supposed to see happy days."

Creeping Death
The moon is down; the night is late
Now come the men, full of hate
Slinking and sliding
Creeping and hiding
Riding their cart of death

Crawling and slipping into their hole
They carry their cargo of death
And out through the wall
Looping and winding
Twisting and turning
They lay their road of death

Now around they turn, and away they run
'til none are left, save just one
He is bent, his body still, and then
Flickering and flashing
Spitting and sparking
Goes the death of other men

It slowly travels that stinking tunnel
Until, at last, it reaches the muzzle
And then, up to the top
Writhing and twisting
Climbing and flinging
Goes the death of other men

And now as the first grey light of dawn
Streaks the eastern sky
There the bodies of other men lie
Who no longer live to die
For that stinking, spitting flame of death

Came at them from below
It laid them dead, the other men
The men we never know.

Steve looked out the driver-side window at the encroaching trees.

Where was Moe sitting when he read that book?

He put down the notebook and closed his eyes. Perhaps his hunting rifle would never feel the same again.

"Rap, rap, rap, blurt," Donnie cried out the sounds of a machine gun. He crouched behind the wagon, swivelling his weapon across the battlefield, mowing down the hated enemy. The gun was a four by four-inch wooden timber, a foot long and made from what had once been a support post for the chain-link fence surrounding George Hartman's tennis court.

The sports site had gradually fallen into disuse although some played tennis for years after the superintendent, Mr. Hartman had left town. By the time Jack Mcbriar had the position in the 1950s, the company had downgraded the position to Foreman, and the tennis court grew derelict. The cast-concrete lawn roller sinking into the clay of the court sometimes provided an excellent shooting position near the creek. Occasionally, one or all of the boys would tug at the heavy steel handle. The massive roller would not budge. By the time they grew larger, older, they had lost interest.

There was lots of old wood left over from the fence when the maintenance gang finally dismantled it. Donnie made the gun barrel from a pair of stilts that someone in town had made. The things had not been popular, and Donnie had scrounged the bits from somewhere. The wedge for the foothold made a credible trigger assembly and the two by two an excellent gun barrel that swivelled neatly on a big spike driven through into the four by four.

Donnie grabbed the wagon tongue and advanced to the laneway past Dad's fall-barren garden, pursuing the fleeing enemy in his makeshift Bren gun carrier. Another burst from the machine gun sealed the fight. Donnie would not cross the road into the ditch and wet marshy area between him and the ice rink. The swampy ground would be a little too close to real Great War conditions. Donnie preferred to play this part in his mind. Many days, Donnie played alone, fighting thousands of enemy and led his division to glorious victory in this sanitized slaughter.

"What's a Bren gun carrier?" Donnie asked.

"Learn about World War Two for that one," Moe said.

"You don't enjoy getting your feet wet and mucky," Moe had other memories of putrid muck that did not involve war.

"It happens lots," Donnie looked at his hands, scrapped and covered in dirt from his slide down the cliff.

Moe looked through the trees to where the creek widened out and eased into the river, near where the big house used to be. The foreman's house was the only one that flooded when the spring runoff was unusually high. Twice in Moe's lifetime, the river had covered the first floor. He remembered the water only ever got to fifty feet of the Hayward back door. It seemed scary.

Donnie beside Monty Mcbriar's Model-A Ford without its headlights near where the creek passes under the back road to Hayward's and Mcbriar's houses. It is late April high water but perhaps not the big flood of 1960.

In summer, the creek formed a lazy meandering estuary there, guarded by fetid forest floor litter and slippery muddy banks, too broad to jump and smelled terrible. The kids seldom played there, perhaps mostly because they found it impossible to leap the stream, humbling them, and mud filled shoes were not the same as sand-filled shoes.

The place did not have a boat mooring, mostly because when logs floated down the river, a small boom guarded the mouth, making the fall rear-end cleanup log drive easier. The steep banks near the river, the result of a levee created in the last gasp of the Spanish being a glacial spillway, made it hard to get near the water and any dock would be further inland in the mosquito-infested creek bottomland.

Donnie headed down the sloping lawn between Mcbriar's house and the river. The creek mouth was fifty feet further downstream. He gingerly descended the slippery gangway, careful to put his running shoes on the wooden-slat treads, and reached the deck of Mcbriar's dock. It was May, and the river ran cold, but this year there was no threat of a high flood. Floods came in May, but the winter had been drier, and they did not need to release Agnew Lake.

The river in flood in May 1960
The dock where Donnie caught the sucker a few years before was just to the right of the leaning tree.

With the worm can and dip net set safely onto the planks, Donnie unwound the black cotton fishing line from his birch pole and slipped a wriggling worm onto the hook. This spring, he had been coming here almost every day after school and found success. They had had several excellent feeds of whitefish he had pulled from this spot. The unusual spring gave Donnie the most rewarding fishing of his life.

Donnie handled the straight birch pole with loving care. Dad had made this for him, with the brown and yellowing bark left intact. Where his hands had worn the pole to a bark-less, smooth finish, Donnie could feel the warm comfort of the wood, even in this chill May air. The line went into the water, with a red and white bobber holding the hook just above the bottom. He would not catch pickerel or bass here, only the bottom feeders. Sometimes Donnie was lucky right away; today the bobber swirled gently on the shore current but stayed high.

Donnie relaxed and looked across the water, still flowing spring-fast although not high. The rushing water was full of threat and yet beckoning as it rushed headlong to disappear beyond the bend downstream from the narrows at the sandpit. He cherished these times, here alone with his thoughts, and the river's far shore dark with black spruce broken by the white trunks of birch. These trees grew at off angles on the steep bank that formed the south shore. White trunks looked like fingers searching for what, Donnie did not know. It was a mysterious place, over there, dark, dangerous and intriguing. He could not wait to be older to explore. Above him, the barren and not yet budding silver maple swayed in the slight breeze. All the stress of being in school, his fears of being bullied, the teacher often unhappy with his work, the other kids always representing social embarrassment, everything faded in this quiet, embracing fishing spot.

The bobber ducked into the water. Donnie pulled gently, wanting to set the hook. Yanking hard or pulling too soon would let the fish get free. The bottom feeders were sluggish, although in the cold springtime water, fish were friskier, and Donnie had learned patience from several failures.

Got it!

The slim pole did not bend. The well-cured birch wood was stiff and not pliable. It would break before it gave much. This fish was more substantial than the ones Donnie usually hooked. He was excited, anticipating a bigger prize and more bragging. He lifted a large, unfamiliar animal from the water. It was more yellow than the whitefish.

Careful

One false move and the fish could fall from the hook and flop into the water. Donnie flourished the hand net, Dad's latest addition to the family fishing gear, and he scrambled to lift the frame beneath the fish and ease struggling animal into the mesh. His knees squeezed around the flopping body and froze it in place so Donnie could finger through the mesh and work the hook free.

Donnie had caught a five-pound sucker. This time of year, it would not taste muddy, and he anticipated the praise and the sound of the fish sizzling in Mom's frying pan. He hurried home as suppertime approached, after a fruitless effort to add to his catch. It was one of the shorter times on the dock, but this prize was worth the reduced solitude.

Cleaning the fish did not attract Donnie, but he had learned this necessary skill from Dad, and he was proud of it.

"If you catch it, you clean it." Dad always said although he made an exception for Mom who had learned from her father how to clean a fish.

A few pages of an old Toronto Star covered the washing line stoop. The grey hand de-scaler deftly moved as Donnie scraped around the dorsal and pectorals and went as near the tail as he could find scales, then up beneath the gills and done. The hunting knife flashed as he severed the head and tail. Donnie carefully slit down the belly avoiding a cut finger or smearing fish poop onto the flesh. He scrapped the guts onto the paper along with the dorsal fin. Donnie could not yet fillet the fish. He would leave that to Mom or Dad. It was too early in the year for the garden hose, so he washed the fish in a pan of water from the kitchen, and it was ready for Mom. The paper neatly wrapped the offal, and in the last act, Donnie buried the package of guts in Dad's garden, deep enough not to attract any scavenging animals. It made the best fertilizer, Dad said. That sucker went into the freezer.

"I caught about thirty whitefish and the sucker that one spring. I never saw another spring with the perfect conditions of that year. It was a special time." Moe smiled at Donnie, at the memory.

"The water was about six feet deep off the dock. The whole river is shallow, and the only deeper spot was the old channel that meanders down the middle of the wide part, where the dams raised the water and flooded the old river floodplain. In summer, the ancient river would have only been ten yards wide. It probably flowed fast though. I saw it twice when they wanted to inspect the power-plant foundations and opened Nairn dam to drain the river. It was nothing but mud and a lot of sunken pine saw-logs from way before they built the dams."

"I've seen that," said Donnie, "it's icky and stinky."

The river had many mysteries, a history that Moe filled in with guesses, and the nature of the company town ensured that no old, grey-haired men sat in the summer sunshine, regaling children with stories of how it was before. The only old person Moe remembered was Mrs. McLennan, Gillis' mother who had been more interested in teaching the Bible than history.

In Moe's childhood, the river had mostly been a vast expanse of blue, rippling into dancing diamonds on a breezy day, beckoning and threatening, a constant companion to the bush and the steep grey hill where he now sat.

"I got a new rod later," Moe frowned. "Once, when I was riding my bike to fish in the tailrace, I caught it in the front wheel. The spokes broke it. I was upset, but Dad just took the end eye and put it on the pole that was left. It worked fine, but it didn't have the reach. That was a sad day, and I felt so silly. I don't think Dad even scolded me about it."

"I hate making mistakes or being wrong," Donnie stared far away. Moe resisted listing the litany of failures that threatened to come to mind.

"That spring, fishing was one of my happy times." Moe tried to focus on the pleasant.

"I love it every time," Donnie, at last, smiled, "on the dock with the birch pole or using my rod and reel in the tailrace."

Chapter Sixteen

Steve set the notebook down. The talk of war and death unsettled him. He opened the photo album, and the first picture he saw was a black and white shot of the town dated 1968. The old school filled the middle ground. Steve looked up, startled. The car had to be right near where that school had been. He got out and looked back, but large mature trees hid the spot from where Moe had made the picture.

They had brushed out all that thought Steve, *maybe for a firebreak and the transmission lines used to run there.*

From the hill at the garages east of town in 1968

He walked towards the bush that came almost to the spot where the car had stopped. For sure, he now stood where the building had been. Steve pushed forward, parting the poplar and aspen walking with the ease of an experienced hunter through the clutching undergrowth and amongst the high ferns.

Somewhere there was the classroom. Moe's desk was right about here.

He looked around at the dense bush.

The things we build can disappear so fast.

Little L is standing near where my desk was for grade six
Steve would see all this greenery.

Steve returned to the car, now eager to look at more photos. Somehow, this old geezer lost on the property drew Steve into another world he could not have imagined. A childhood story came to mind.

Through the wardrobe, Steve looked at the old maroon car. *I hope no evil witches are waiting for me, but this is someone's Narnia.*

He stared at the picture once more. White houses, neatly laid out filled the distance past the school, and before the hills beyond the river. The next photo was a high shot of the town, labelled August 1968, in colour, of those same white houses, running between the hill and the river. It looked like a place everyone would want to live.

High Falls, August 1968

He returned to the notebook and read. "Growing up in High Falls, except for the school, was wonderful until high school and the end of my youth. The distance, 20 miles to town made a social life hard, almost impossible. High school liberated me, and I liked school again. That didn't matter when I was young. The play was the big thing."

Donnie tore around the corner of the house. He and some others were playing a pursuit game, like ally-ally-over without the ball. Donnie dashed for the gap between the woodshed and Dad's shop. Just as he got there, Lucky, who had been playing the game with the kids came charging, unseen from the opposite direction. Donnie and Lucky met full speed in the gap. The dog was quicker and jumped up, as he often did to greet Donnie, but the force of their impact sent Donnie reeling backwards.

"Oh," Donnie collapsed onto the dirt path in front of the woodshed door.

Lucky seemed no worse for wear, but Donnie sat on the ground, hunched over with the wind knocked out of him. It was one of life's lessons, taught without compromise.

"That wasn't the way to learn about inertia and momentum," Moe chuckled. Donnie stared back with uncomprehending eyes.

"Don't worry, kid," you'll learn about physics soon enough.

"I already know about physics," Donnie seemed defensive, "and that crash sure hurt. I'm glad Lucky never gets hurt."

Moe's thoughts turned to the dog. Lucky was a constant factor in his childhood, the one who always loved and made Donnie feel better, never questioning or scolding, full of joy.

The kids struggled waist deep in loose powdery snow. The winter had enticed them to the base of No. 1 dam, and they had come up from the power plant along the winter-stilled log sluice. Everyone was intent on the fight to move in the deep drifts. Lucky seemed to enjoy the experience. Gasping for breath, Donnie stopped to watch the dog leap into the powder. Suddenly, Lucky stopped and cocked his head followed by a leap into the air, and a nose-first dive into the drift. He almost disappeared, but then his head rose like a porpoise in the sea and, with a flip tossed the body of a mouse high into the air.

"Wow," Donnie cried. Lucky was not too far from being a wolf after all.

"Lucky loved Mom the most," Moe said. "He once leapt into the river and followed the boat with Dad rowing and Mom in the rear seat, all the way to the swimming hole, about a kilometre. We thought Lucky would walk around with us, but he had other plans."

"Another time, we wanted to go somewhere and leave him home, so we hooked the screen porch door to keep him in. When Mom walked away, Lucky charged right through the screen. He was afraid she would leave him. He lived with us for about eight years." Moe frowned at his memory of Lucky's end.

"I am sad," said Donnie, "I cry and cry and cry, every time he dies in my arms."

"He died in my arms, right by our back steps. I cried all night." Moe relived that terrible moment and still felt like crying.

"He gave us a splendid gift," Donnie sounded wise. "Lucky said goodbye. I know he heard our tears."

"Yes," said Moe reluctantly as if he still wanted to hold the dog and keep Lucky's life-fire going. "I know that now, but then it just hurt… hurt badly. Dad put his body in the shop, gently on an old rug. I had to go to school the next day, the first day of high school and in itself, a big fear. Before going to the bus, I went into the shop and petted him. He was cold, and it didn't help. I had never had a loved one die before."

"Dad never marked the spot where he buried Lucky under the big cedars on the other side of the creek; the place Hartman buried two of his dogs."

"I visit there a lot," said Donnie. "We play all along the creek there, a stinky mucky place but it's shady and quiet. Lucky sleeps there without being disturbed."

"He taught me how to grieve when he died. He taught me that, in the end, it isn't the loss but the memories that keep living. Those memories of Lucky have always felt good over the years. I still remember, still love, and still miss him. When Dad and Mom died later, Lucky's memories helped."

"Mom and Dad die?" Donnie seemed almost ready to cry. There was a sob.

"Dad taps a few maple trees over there for maple syrup," Donnie reached for a happier topic. "In April I drag the toboggan with a big kettle on it, collecting the sap."

"We have a couple of steel spiles, but Dad made a bunch out of some red-pine boards. They work well."

"There was a big maple that would take two spiles, right near the river. Usually, we finished tapping before the river came up too high and we couldn't get at the tree. I remember emptying a bucket standing in river water. It was always fun doing that, but hard work too," Moe said, "especially when I was smaller. I miss all that now."

"I still do it most springs," said Donnie. "Once in a while, the river is up a bit wanting to flood my boots... collecting that one bucket."

Moe's scepticism of Donnie grew.

Is this kid trying to worm into my memories?

A flash of light startled Moe down to his left. He could see his car and a young man poking around it, actually sitting on the hood and reading.

My notes, Moe thought with amusement. *He'll never understand.*

An understanding was coming to Steve. He could see how, in old age, someone might want to return to their place of youth, and this must have been a beautiful spot to live as a kid.

Steve thought about his place of growing up. He was a town kid but had learned to love the outdoors, hunting, fishing and canoeing. Steve and his wife, Deb had eagerly moved to the older house along the regional road near the Vermillion River. Yes, he could have comfortably lived in High Falls.

Steve read on.

"Opposite the school, at the base of the big hill was an enormous boulder. I'm not sure it was from when they built the railway trestle or a glacial erratic, but a whip-poor-will nested near there and every evening it sang the sun down. I remember one evening standing on the high road near the bridge and shining a spotlight on the rock, the only time I ever saw the bird. It seemed grey and the size of a mourning dove, but then I'm not sure. You could hear its echo everywhere. It rivalled the call of the loons on the river towards the rapids."

Right over there, Steve thought and eased away from the car to the roadway before the culvert. He could make out a big boulder through the entanglement. He stood and stared for a long time, trying to remember the last time he had heard a whip-poor-will.

Steve turned to look towards the abandoned town-site, trying to ignore the industrial mayhem that had replaced the houses. He could imagine the haunting evening call reaching to the river, the gentle darkness of a lingering summer evening settling upon the place. He could believe that echo would bring a child home.

"We have to go home and check in when the lights come on," Donnie said. "When we are older, we stay out after that and play hide and seek and stuff."

"There was never any thought of danger," Moe reflected. "Everyone knew and trusted everyone else, even if they didn't always like each other."

"Mom used to blow a whistle at suppertime," Moe remembered.

"The kids tease us about that. I wish Mom would stop it." Donnie frowned.

"She did, eventually," Moe replied, "but being late for supper was a big no-no."

"She stopped blowing the whistle?" Donnie seemed sceptical.

"I tried living in the city," Moe wandered on, "but I couldn't raise the kids there. I grew up here, the opposite of what you need to know to keep your kids safe in Toronto. There were too many strangers."

"We rarely have strangers move in," said Donnie, "but new ones come, and eventually we make friends. Lots of us grow up together, some of the old families like Mom's and the new ones. For kids, it doesn't matter. I think adults find it harder."

"My friend Bucky moved away," his voice had a sad note.

Donnie walked up the short incline to Bucky's house, the big one on the corner that was once the boarding house, serving meals to the workers living in the clubhouse. Mrs. Mcquillen stood at the back door hanging washing that would soon dry in the morning sun.

"Is Bucky here?" Donnie asked shyly. He was only six years old.

Mrs. Mcquillen was a big, friendly woman with a loud laugh and a smile.

"Bucky, Donnie's here." She took the clothespins from her mouth long enough to call her son. Bucky crashed through the doorway, slapping the door against his mother.

"Watch that, I'm supposed to spank you," she chuckled. Bucky hurried down the steps.

"Look at the dew on the cellar door," Donnie exclaimed. Bucky led the way, carefully climbing up the slippery cover beside the door hinges.

"You first," he said. Donnie braced himself like a surfer and pushed off with his hind foot, sliding easily down the dew-covered grey painted outside cellar door that sloped to the driveway. He almost made it to the bottom before his feet found their wind, slipped out from under him and planted his bum firmly on the wet wood. He and Bucky laughed, as Bucky flew past and landed clumsily on the gravel. Sliding down the cellar door was a morning ritual whenever the dew was right. After a couple more slides, they had dried the surface, and the game ended.

Bucky with Grandma and us about 1950

"McCartneys took over the boarding house," Donnie added. "My teacher lives there." He suddenly looked eight years old. "Her name is Joan. She's very young, and I think she likes boys. The older ones, the ones who they held back a grade, all sit at the front of the room."

Moe smiled. "She couldn't live in the clubhouse. It was hard to heat in the winter with that coal-fired convection furnace, and men stayed there from time to time. That would be scandalous."

"What's scandalous," asked Donnie. He had no problem with where the boys might sit, or his teacher live. At his age, girls were friends and foes only.

"They tease me about being young and small," Donnie sighed.

"They are only kids," said Moe. "We all grow up."

"It makes me sad."

"I know it did," said Moe. "Just try to be nice to everyone."

"I just try to be invisible as much as I can," Donnie fidgeted and seemed to look for something through the trees.

Brian lifted the cover to the little window where coal went into the clubhouse cellar. Even if they had locked the front door, this was always open. He slipped into the darkness, followed by Donnie and several others. The clubhouse crawl space was a warm, dry place to play.

"I'll get the lights," Donnie felt his way up the stairs, opened the door into the poolroom for some light and found the switch. The one bare bulb flared, lighting the cellar and the enormous barrel of a furnace with its colossal convection heat pipes. It was usually only used when someone stayed. Otherwise, the water taps in the washrooms ran a trickle to prevent freezing. Water came free from the dam and never short.

Brian twisted the clinker grate, just for fun and the kids made their way behind the contraption and climbed the board half-wall into the darker crawl space full of dusty sand that hadn't seen water in decades.

"Watch out," Donnie said, "there's some wood there with nails." These were a significant danger here. The kids spent a good hour crawling about, exploring in the dusty sand. Mothers never seemed to complain, and Donnie never wondered if they knew what the kids had been doing. Boredom or hunger usually ended the journey into the mysterious world.

"I can't remember how many times we did that," Moe rubbed his beard.

"Lots, we do it lots," Donnie replied.

Chapter Seventeen

Steve wanted to get out and explore, maybe keep looking, but he needed to be at the gate when the OPP and the Regionals arrived.

This old guy knows this place better than I do, Steve thought. *If he is hiding deliberately, I wouldn't know where to look.*

Steve walked around and stared into the bush, past where the school had stood, and he wandered to where he could see down the rough road to the river where visitors who did not trespass might get to the water. Someone had used it this summer but not recently although he noticed what might have been moose tracks crushing the grass. He looked behind nervously. No one wanted to be exposed, if a bull moose in rut materialized in September.

Where are the damned cops? Steve checked his watch. Light would soon fade, and darkness quickly came as fall approached.

Steve retrieved his binoculars from the pickup, swept the work site, and up the hill. He slowly passed over where Moe and Donnie lingered, but the thick autumn leaves hid all. Steve never hunted until the brutal winds and rain or an early snowfall stripped the branches. Moe did not see Steve's pass with the glasses. He and Donnie were busy getting wet.

They stood with Mom just outside the back door of No. 1 power plant. The log sluice ran full, and the men high above pushed the wood towards the spot where the flowing water, smooth and dark except for the jack pine floaters suddenly disappeared. It turned into a foaming rush as it headed to the lower river into the tailrace. The more massive logs shot rooster-tails high into the air and soaking streams of water washed both sides. The trick was to pick a lull in the big ones and run for it past the corner of the plant to the dry safety of the far path. Sometimes, a log to jumped from the chute high above their heads. Being hit would be fatal.

"Go," Mom cried, and a dozen little feet surged beneath the concrete and shot towards safety. Most times, they did not escape without a small shower soaking their towels. Many times, they only reached the safe space under the sluice and had to wait for the next brief opportunity. Water always dripped from the chute, and there were enough splashes to make water run in a stream beneath. The kids shrieked and laughed. This place made an excursion to the swimming hole an adventure.

"Is everyone okay?" Mom always asked. Donnie thought she enjoyed this as much as the kids did. When she had been a kid in High Falls, this sluice was not here, and they had to pick their way over the original log chute dug into the dirt further inland.

Pike men are pushing logs into No. 1 log sluice 1950s

Fun, remembered Moe, *too bad it's gone.*

"That log sluice is the only time I get a smack on the bum from Dad," Donnie seemed both upset and proud. As if it were maybe a sign that he had done something rebellious.

"I'm too young to know better," Donnie continued, "and neither does John.."

"In 1948," added Moe, "I was not even two then."

"I'm two when this happens," Donnie ignored Moe's intrusion into his story, "and I'm so interested in the big machinery, the trucks and all the men. We wander over the bridge, something they forbid us to do without an adult, and they tell us to stay away."

Moe had closed his eyes with the memories and listened to Donnie. The kid sounded young.

"The big cement mixer is the scariest and most interesting thing. Men shovel sand and bags of grey stuff into a big scoop while a noisy engine turns an enormous barrel. Then the scoop lifts on big arms and dumps the dry stuff in while water is gushing in with it. After a bit, they open a chute on the far side, and guys with strong arms take a full wheel-barrow load of goopy grey stuff, push it up a high ramp and over the big pipes to where they are building something."

"They were building the log sluice," Moe helped.

"I know that," snapped Donnie. "I remember we go there with Dad sometimes when they aren't working, and he shows us the wooden boxes."

"Forms," added Moe, raising another scowl from the kid.

"I see they chipped the old concrete at the bottom of a box. Dad says it's so the next concrete will stick to it better. He says it's something useful to know."

"Mom always comes and gets us from over the bridge. Boy, she is mad." Donnie looked very uncomfortable. "Her scolding frightens me, but when we get home Dad, taking the leather strap and giving us two good ones is worse."

"It's the only time I can remember," said Moe. "The strap always hung there inside the cellar door frame, threatening if we misbehaved."

"It still does," Donnie shuddered, "but we get brave enough to do it. I love that enormous machine."

"One thing Dad said about his growing up; he was living at the Aurora-Lloydtown Road, the Sixth Line of King Township, and he would ride his bike up to Highway 9 to watch the steam-dredge when they dug the canal at the Holland Marsh. I think he was as interested in building the log sluice as we were."

Through a break in the trees, Moe could make out the shattered remains of the disused log sluice past the dark penstocks. The wetting at the log sluice got him thinking about other water episodes. With the river, the lake and the frog pond a central part of life, the children found many chances for getting wet feet and more.

There were mostly unwritten rules and taboos, Moe remembered. No *one had a fence, we could run anywhere, but we knew you did not go into people's vegetable gardens or damage anything. The town imposed a cheap price for freedom. McCartney started a four-hole pitch and putt golf course, and Eversheds kept it going. It circled Evershed's house and touched Moir's.*

Moe could feel the putter in his hand. *Most people played with only a putter to hit the 50 yards to the hole.*

Eversheds lived across the street from us. Warren was my age, Bobby older, went to Gaza with the Canadian force in the United Nations and then came back to complete high school and drove the school bus while he did it. The damn bus was cold in winter, Moe shivered, *because Bobby, being across the street didn't have time to let it warm up before we got on, minus 45 Fahrenheit that one morning. Bobby had that Volkswagen Beetle with no windshield defroster... wild rides in that in winter.*

Warren discovered the secret trapdoor in my shack, Moe smiled. *He showed us why, when you hide a dugout you don't nail a chair to the hatch cover.*

Why didn't Warren and I become best friends? Perhaps Kelvin signed on first, and it's hard for kids to have three-way friendships. We became better friends much later in life, but cruel fate snatched that away when Warren died. Moe felt more sadness of loss. *He had honoured both Kelvin and Warren's names in a story he wrote.*

Moe considered the great things he and Kelvin had done.

Donnie and Kelvin were footloose. It was a warm July morning, with no one else around. They made their way along the river, at the edge of Evershed's backyard and down the hill to the dock at the little bay beside No. 2 tailrace. As was usual in the summer, not much water flowed between the morning and afternoon shift change times.

"What do you want to do?" Kelvin led the way over the little gangway onto the dock. Donnie thought Eversheds owned the dock although Cummings had a boat there too and maybe someone else.

Donnie looked at the water. "I think we should go for a dip." He smiled mischievously.

"No way," Kelvin exclaimed. "There are no adults here, and we don't have our suits."

"I know," giggled Donnie. "It's totally against the rules. Let's jump in, in our clothes."

It was a suggestion of rebellion too delicious to resist. Breaking two adult rules at the same time. "We're old enough and can swim. The water isn't even over our heads."

"I don't know," Kelvin sounded scared, "Mom wouldn't like it."

Kelvin's mom was bedridden; the lingering effects of polio and Kelvin loved and respected her. Donnie liked her, and he loved his mom too, but this promised freedom.

"Let's do it. We'll be dry before lunch." Donnie was not altogether a brave radical.

Two boys leapt from the dock into the calm water where they had swum with official sanction under adult supervision many times before. The place was a handy alternative to the long trek to the swimming hole near the rapids.

The pair did not frolic, nor make noise, but they soon scrambled, feeling pleasurable guilt back onto the rough planking. The dock slumped on its barrel floaters as they hung from the edge.

"That was fun," Kelvin had found the spirit of the defiant act. "Rules are everywhere," he scoffed, but rose and nervously looked around for any disapproving adult eyes.

"The rules only existed in our heads but kept us safe all those years," Moe said to Donnie. "Nobody died."

Why do people have to break the rules? Steve wondered. *This guy is probably dead.*

Shadows filled the valley, with the police nowhere in sight, and hunger gnawed at Steve.

"Honey," Steve called his wife. It was near quitting time. "Pack me a little lunch and bring it to High Falls. I have to wait here for the cops. An old guy trespassed and is missing."

"I'll make a picnic and bring the kids. Too bad it isn't swimming weather, but they will enjoy it. Daddy's work always excites them. Give me an hour."

It was a half hour drive from home. Steve laughed at the thought of his kids. His daughter was six, and little Stephen was four. To them, he was a hero guarding things against terrorists, or aliens, or zombies. Unfortunately, he was not in the mood to trick them when they arrived. His hunger and worry dominated. If they found a body, he would make sure Deb had them away from it all.

Steve returned to the notebook.

What was this guy doing at that age? He snuck over bridges and played in places that are off limits to anyone but authorized workers with proper safety gear and training. What a different world that was.

Steve found an energy bar on the car seat and satisfied his hunger. Hopefully, Debbie would bring some of her famous chicken-salad sandwiches. She was a down-to-earth type who preferred cooking to partying. He wondered if the security chick measured up. Pierre was as basic a guy as Steve, hunting, fishing and even though he rented somewhere, he often visited Steve's house helping to build something.

As if on cue his cell rang, "private number".

Maybe the cops,

"Hello hot shot, have you found him yet? It's Andrea."

"I told you not to call me at home," Steve tried a joke to cover the growing unease. "Why did you take my number home?"

"If this Pierre turns out to be an axe murderer, I want my ghost to tell the police who's at fault." Andrea giggled. "What's wrong? You sound stressed?"

"It's getting late, and the cops aren't here yet."

"Call the office. They will know, but they said they were on their way."

"Thanks, call Pierre tonight."

"What's the rush? Do you owe this guy money and are using me as a payoff?"

"Maybe I don't like him, and you are revenge."

"Funny man, call me when you know." Andrea punched off, and Steve put the cell into his pocket.

"We used to have to phone from the little booth in the clubhouse," Moe said. "The No. 1 operator had to put us through to the outside line by plugging in a wire. I saw Dad doing it, just like in the old movies. There was no long distance, only local to Copper Cliff and Sudbury."

Dad at No. 1 switchboard
The telephone plug ins are in front of him, and the radio is just visible to
the right. The operator filled in that log sheet every half hour.

"I'm too little to use it, but I see Mom crank the handle
on the brown box and lift the black thing to talk to the
operator in No. 1. He connects the black phone with the
rotary dial. Mom talks to Aunt Ethel. It's complicated to
me."

"It seemed complicated," Moe agreed, "Mutual and
Oxford exchanges."

*All the young people I know don't know how to work
an old dial phone.*

"We mostly send and receive letters and cards," said
Donnie. "I like those nice stamps on the letters. We pick
them up at Mrs. Mackenzie's store."

"They put the big green mailboxes in the clubhouse
front porch after Mrs. Mackenzie closed the store and
moved out. We switched from Turbine post office to
Worthington then. There were no more rides to meet the
milk and mail train. I still have the old combination lock we

had on our box. It's the only numbers I remember from childhood. I still use it 60 years later."

Donnie did not seem to listen. He looked far away.

Mr. Lammi's Jeep truck bounced along hurrying past the dump and towards Turbine Junction. He drove every day to pick up the mail and milk from the local train that went to Little Current each morning and back at night.

Donnie and several of the kids rode in the back, experiencing the bouncing and rough ride of a vehicle built for work, not comfort.

"Look at the car there," Brian leapt from the back of the Jeep almost before Mr. Lammi had stopped. The dust was thick in the air. "I bet it has coal in it."

A gondola car sat on the little siding that had once led to the spur line that had built High Falls. The old railroad bed paralleled the High Falls road, and the kids had once walked it all the way from the garbage dump to the timber structure where the torn down trestle to Big Eddy had begun, right near Insley's house and the car garages.

Donnie explored along the tracks and found an abandoned railway spike. He reached the switch at the head of the siding and looked uncomprehendingly at the railway apparatus, the frog and other mysteries.

"Put the spike on the rail and let's watch the engine squash it," Brian was inventive. Donnie placed the spike carefully on the rail so the engine wheel would hit it.

"Do you think it's safe doing that?" Donnie was nervous. He didn't want to cause a train wreck. The group spent a few minutes discussing the issue and eventually the spike ended up in Donnie's pocket. He felt relieved. Someone found a small stone, and it occupied the spike's spot.

Albert and Mabel Prentice seated on their front steps about 1922
With aunts Ethel and Dorothy
The railway trestle to Big Eddy is visible beyond the houses

The train was late. John led the group up the little hill to the lip of another sand pit. Here, the soft sand let them safely jump and roll down to the bottom. It was one of the best-loved places at Turbine junction.

Stubby ferns that thrived in sunny, dry conditions covered the sand plain and protected the blueberry plants generous offering of fruit. The time passed quickly while the children gorged.

The long rising and falling of the steam whistle called them back to the Jeep. The engineer blew the warning for the highway crossing at Desjardin's farm. Their favourite part was watching the big black engine, billowing smoke charge around the curve from the highway crossing. The steam whistle shrilled, and the bell clanged as the train approached the High Falls' road, and air brakes hissed as it ground to a stop.

The kids strained to watch the front wheels convert the stone on the tracks to powder. The baggage car stopped precisely at Lammi's Jeep with a trainman standing in the open doorway, holding a mail sack. It dropped off first, and one of the bigger boys grabbed it and put it into the truck cab. Lammi reached up and took the first milk crate, gently placing it into the back. Three more followed. They would all go to Mrs Mackenzie's store. There was a carton of bread, and a few boxes addressed to Mr. Mcbriar.

The trainman smiled and waved at the excited youngsters and then grabbed a handhold as the engine drive wheels turned. They spun once in a flurry of sparks and steam and then caught traction. The conductor stood on the bottom step of the lone passenger coach, waving at the engineer and then the children as the mysterious, powerful machine sped up to the west towards Nairn Centre.

Donnie had gotten on the train here, twice. The first time was a trip with Dad and John all the way to Espanola to pick up the old car Dad left in Wilf Lachance's garage for repairs. The other was a 25-cent ride to Nairn Centre to get to a hockey game with Mr Gilbeau, the coach. These adventurous rides guaranteed Donnie's lifetime love of trains. One short toot of farewell from the engine man as the train clanked away. The kids hopped in amongst the crates, and Mr. Lammi headed back to town.

"Look, a bottle broke," Brian exclaimed. The truck bounced too much despite Lammi's caution and the glass milk bottles, rattling noisily in wooden crates with wire cages separating the bottles, succumbed to an unusually large bump where the township had not adequately graded the spring heaved clay. A trail of milk headed to oblivion onto the road, beneath the rear drop gate. Mr. Lammi would have to hose out the truck back at No. 1. The Jeep sped on. The mishap might happen a few times a year.

"That was my favourite summer pastime," Moe shifted on the rock. With the declining sun, the air began to chill and take Moe's body with it.

Debbie Warwick beat the police by half an hour. She pulled her minivan up behind the maroon car. Steve had backed the company truck between Moe's vehicle and the fence.

"Daddy," the kids scrambled out and ran for their usual reward of hugs and air throws. They eventually ended up one in each of their father's arms. Steve noticed his daughter had grown a little too heavy for him to hold in one arm.

"Let's eat. I'm starving," Steve dropped the children onto the blanket Debbie had spread out over the ferns. The kids lasted for one half-sandwich and an Oreo before they headed off to adventure. They had only ever been here with their parents once. They explored the shrubs, trees, and ferns where the school had once been.

"Daddy," his boy called, "I'm in the jungle."

Steve laughed. His son stood in what would have been the school classroom. Steve finally ate a famous chicken salad sandwich, but the kids were too much.

"Don't get lost in there. There might be gorillas."

Even at their age, the kids would not buy that story.

Steve paused, suddenly aware that at one time kids played all around here with abandon. It somehow satisfied that his kids enjoyed some of that fun.

"You haven't found him yet," Debbie noticed her husband's suddenly serious look.

"I haven't been looking, just reading and waiting for the cops," Steve held up Moe's notebook. "It's interesting stuff. The old guy grew up here and tells a fascinating story. It must have been a glorious life here for kids."

"You have a soft heart, Steve Warwick. I got me a good one," Deb watched her kids trying to climb a poplar tree.

"Reading this, it's almost like I grew up here." Steve glanced at the sky, now noticeably darkening towards sunset colours. "I hope the cops get here soon. I hope he isn't dead. His name's Maurice Hayward."

Debbie leafed through the notebook and photos while Steve ate. She paused often.

"I hope we can meet him," she said in a low whisper. "I want to hear more."

"Who won the ball game?" Steve suddenly returned to the present.

"I'll never tell," Deb laughed, "because I don't watch kid's games and don't know. It's on the PVR."

Debbie looked to where her children played a hiding game in the ferns.

"Good thing you're an excellent cook," Steve retaliated. "I might be here all night."

The OPP cruiser sped around the bend and slid to a stop on the roadway.

"Sorry we took long," a short female constable emerged from the driver's side. She wore corporal's stripes. A gangly young man who looked like the rookie he was, walked from the far side.

"There was a rollover near the Vermillion, and we had to wait for EMS and another car. What's the story? You have a missing person?"

"I miss this place," Moe sighed.

"I never want to leave," said Donnie. "It's my home."

"I built a shack under the big elm tree," Moe wandered back, "and it took me over two years, mostly by myself."

"Kelvin comes over and helps, sometimes," Donnie said, "but at first it was all me. I am happy. I get to decide everything."

"Yes, I was in total control," Moe said, "made all the decisions and had to solve every problem by myself."

Moe fell silent and thought about it all, the satisfaction of doing, the challenges and the loneliness of not having anyone to share the excitement.

"I learned a lot of problem-solving," he went on, "but I didn't learn to share and cooperate. Even now, I have trouble accepting other ideas when I have a plan in my head. It drives the wife nuts. She has good ideas."

"Dad and Mom work together," Donnie said. "The heavy lifting is the worst part, but also the best solutions I invent. I make the roof from one of the big heavy doors from the garage where I hear Dad swear. It is too heavy for me to lift, but I get it done every time."

"You're busier than I was," said Moe, "I only had to do that once. Somehow, that door was special, and I had to use it. I can still see the flaking green paint on the barn-board."

"I build the frame using pulpwood posts and tie them together with cross beams and then brace the far side," Donnie ignored Moe and sounded proud. "Then I lean two more pulpwood sticks against the posts and flip that big door over the ground until it is lying flat on those angled logs. Then I throw my old frayed big rope with the log-hook on its end over the top from the far side. The hook goes on the bottom edge of the door, and I tie the other to Dad's old firewood sawhorse. I make it stay on an angle on two feet, just so it will hold a big pulp log, the heaviest I can lift into the cradle and pull it back, so the weight of the log is stretching the rope. Then I go to the far side, grab the bottom edge of the door, and push it up the ramp. The sawhorse and log on the far side fall back to the flat, but while they do, it's like I have other hands shoving the door. It goes a few inches at a time, and then I reset and do it over."

"Like the Egyptians building the pyramids," Moe smiled.

"I never think of that, but just about getting the door on top for the roof. I get it done every time."

How many times have I thought about this in my lifetime? Moe wondered.

Donnie stood on top of the shack, hammering a railing around the L-shaped structure. It had grown nicely, and it was his pride and joy. The last thing would be to add this railing for a top deck, and then he would have finished.

Dad worked in the potato patch, cleaning up the vines and debris after the harvest. Donnie hoped the little shack impressed him.

"You need to stop building that," Dad snapped. "Don't do any more. You're working too hard."

Donnie flared. The place was part of him, part of his self-worth.

The only time Dad says anything about it is to tell me to stop.

Donnie did not analyze his feelings or motives, but in the end, he had been building the whole thing looking for praise from his father. Donnie did not consider that perhaps Dad remembered another little 11-year-old boy who, in 1921, had to work hard to earn room and board. Maybe his Dad could not find the words to express his pain and hardship and only wanted to spare his son the same fate.

The words cut into Donnie, and he became angry. It had not occurred to him he had been building this to impress his Dad, and now he felt condemned. His anger boiled over, washing away any sense. Donnie did not have the strength to argue, but acted out his feelings.

Whack, whack, whack

The hammer flew against the wood as he hammered apart the work he had just moments before proudly assembled. He worked away until suppertime, and the next day after school, he began on the old main shack. By week's end it was all flat, gone, done, all the hard, satisfying work, and the material piled up for something Donnie did not know.

It was a long, desolate winter with the shack no longer visible from the house and no longer a secret place to retreat to in the snow.

Kelvin Dunne with the shack in front of the big elm tree and the foreman's house in the background

The grief ended, and by late spring, Donnie had hatched a plan. He would build a new shack out of sight of criticism. He and Kelvin would make it across the river.

Moe frowned at the still raw memory, after all these years, still tugging at his heart. He tried to lighten the mood.

"Archimedes had nothing on us," Moe said.

"What, who's Archimedes?"

"You'll learn about that," Moe answered. "I became an amateur engineer before an amateur scientist; you will too."

Donnie beamed with pride, accepting the praise.

Chapter Eighteen

"**Y**ou've done all you could," the corporal told Steve, sitting beside him as he headed the company pickup back to the gate. With Moe still missing, it was faint praise. He had given the police a tour of the site from Big Eddy dam to No. 1 and through the flats to the river.

"This is too big. We need more boots on the ground and a helicopter, and," the cop hesitated, "a dive team. He might be in the water. I'll call for backup but," again she paused, "it's getting dark, and the forecast is for near freezing tonight. We need to find the guy fast or..." Her voice trailed off. She had seen many searches bad outcomes.

"I'll call my boss," Steve said. "At least we can start by checking the intakes in No. 1 and No. 2. I need the maintenance gang for that."

"We can't have a helicopter until morning," the corporal said, "but they are sending six officers and are calling out the volunteer search teams. It will be well past dark. Where can I set up a command spot? The van is on its way."

"It's five o'clock on a Sunday," Steve's boss snarled through the phone. He had been about to sit down to a family dinner. "That's overtime."

"I know," Steve said, "but the cops are bringing in a dive team, and we need to make sure the racks are clear. I need two guys and have the substation to back off the generators when they are working."

Steve was not sure how familiar his new boss was with procedures. The young guy had little experience, none on the ground and the rumour was he knew someone higher up. The company considered overseeing the power plants as a starter management job.

"We need to find this guy," Steve pushed. "It's going to be cold tonight, and he might not last. He's old."

"Okay, but don't think you're getting any overtime out of this." It seemed his boss wanted to assert his authority. Steve decided not to argue. His job description and union rules would eventually make his boss do the right thing.

"I want to land the helicopter down that street on the helipad by the river," Corporal Sing said, "the dive team can work from there too, and we will set up the command post by that Quonset building."

She was logical. Overhead wires would not be an issue, and there was easy river access.

"Do you have any guesses where he could be?"

Moe's mind wandered all over his old home. One minute they were swimming at the little beach near the rapids, the next they were digging a canal to cut across an oxbow in the creek below the school.

Damned silly, he thought, *messing with nature's way there. We were ignorant.*

"It's fun," said Donnie, "we get to do something real."

"I was here a few years ago," said Moe, "and I could still find the ditch we dug."

Donnie and Kelvin struggled up the steep bank, dragging shovels. They had beached the red rowboat on the narrow strip of sand below, tied firmly to a root. Pulp logs floated nearby. The log drive had switched from using the High Falls log chute to sending the wood through the fore bay dam and over the falls.

Dora Dunne watched from her bed in the back bedroom of the cottage that was the last house at the river. The river, the hills and the rapids were her constant daily view, and now Donnie and her son Kelvin gave her something new to watch.

"Mom, can watch us here," Kelvin said as he struggled up the bank with a salvaged board. The boys kept the project a secret, out of sight and criticism of parents and meddling friends.

It took all summer. The boys worked harder than paid help would have done, day after day until they had dug a ten by ten-foot hole, five feet deep, nestled nicely amongst the birch trees and entirely hidden unless someone came right up to it. They lined the hole with dozens of four-inch pulpwood logs, borrowed from the river. They made the roof from the doors floated across on a bigger old wooden motorboat that had no motor. Somewhere, they scrounged a cast-iron stove, and it ended up inside this new, buried shack. It never got a chimney nor ever lighted, but it was a point of pride for Kelvin and Donnie.

The project lasted for two glorious summers, with the boys making exotic plans for a telephone and a cable car from what the townsfolk called "the point" to the headland where they buried the shack. The planning, romance, imagination made for some wonderfully sharing times as they idled in the shade at the riverbank. Alas, nothing could come of it. Scrounging only went so far, and the bits of aluminium electrical transmission cable they found would only go a quarter of the way across.

Their attempts to beg a telephone receiver to connect the shack to Kelvin's house led to a friendly refusal from Vince Houlahan, then assistant foreman, as he patiently explained how phones worked and how anything lying around would not work. The kindly twinkle in Vince's eyes softened Donnie's disappointment.

Donnie had the impression that Vince would have joined in the fun if he could become 13 again.

While building the river shack Donnie came close to death, or at least serious injury.

"We're nearly done," Donnie and Kelvin sat on top of a platform, a sort of high dock protruding from the riverbank at their landing spot. It was part of their idea of the cable car link across the river.

"I'll just hammer in these last spikes," Donnie swung his hammer, driving six-inch nails through some pulpwood to complete the deck where it hung six feet above the shallow water.

"Oh," Donnie cried as the deck suddenly gave way. The fall was sudden; he did not have time to think, or be afraid or do anything. Instantly, he hung upside down, dangling from his legs hooked over the pulpwood crossbar halfway down. His head swung just above the water, and the hammer waved from his extended right hand. Kelvin, who had been sitting on the shore-end of the deck, clung to an upright with his legs flat on the collapsed logs that now ran on a steep slope to the river.

Hysteria hit and both boys erupted in uncontrolled laughter. The fear had come after the swift disaster. Only then did they both know how close Donnie had come to being hurt, or worse.

Thinking about it later, Donnie figured it might have been a good thing. If the platform had survived, the river loggers doing their fall clean up would have known someone appropriated their wood. Instead, the remains of the project ended up as part of the shack, safely out of sight from the river.

By the next summer, things had changed, and in the fall, Donnie went off to high school. His friendship with Kelvin two years younger waned, and soon the building site became lonely, almost forgotten seasons of fun.

Moe jerked back from his memories of those glorious days crossing the river. He felt his hip twinge and a cramp in his bum. He stood to stretch. The air grew colder. The lights of a large vehicle passed along the roadway and turned to a stop almost directly below. Moe shivered slightly.

Maybe I should go now.

Instead, not wanting to get into a confrontation with people upset he had trespassed, Moe pulled a thin thermal blanket from his pack, found a softer spot beside the juniper bush and lay down. Somehow, the pungent aroma reassured and warmed him. He offered a trail bar to Donnie.

"I'm not hungry", Donnie said.

"Shouldn't you be getting home? Your mom will be worried."

"I need to stay with you," Donnie replied and lay beside the old man. Donnie was so slight that Moe could not feel him, but he knew he was there. It seemed as if he had always been there. September shadows deepened, cloaking the pair in the gloom.

Steve sent Deb and the children home before dark. He and the rookie constable worked their way down the little creek from the gate until they reached the river. No disturbance in the grass suggested that anyone had recently passed. They headed back along the roadway, skirting the ring bus and arrived at the turnaround just as the OPP command van pulled up in front of the Quonset.

"We've lost most of the light," Corporal Sing said to the Sergeant in charge. "We need infrared."

"I'll see if someone from tactical can run out some night vision goggles. It's getting cold. Any chance we know where to look?"

"I already looked in the obvious and easy places," Steve said. "I'm waiting for a couple of workers to help check the trash racks. If he went into the fore bay, the flow would likely suck the body against the bars."

"Not good," the cop frowned.

Steve yawned.

"You look beat", Sing felt tired herself but had been on long days before. "Go lie down in the van until your guys arrive."

"Personally," Steve said. "I don't think he's in the water or dead. I was looking through his stuff. This guy grew up here and knows a lot of the surrounding bush. I'm betting he's at some favourite spot and holed up for the night. I hope he's warm."

Steve went inside the command post and found the cot. His long day finally hit, and he drifted off, glad he wasn't shivering in the bush.

Chapter Nineteen

Moe eased into sleep. The chill made him drowsy, and he realized he had not had his customary afternoon nap. Sleep led to dreams, and the chilled air turned his dreams to winter. *Snow,* Moe thought, as he drifted into sleep, *snow and cold and fun.*

"Lots of fun," said Donnie.

Is Donnie in my dreams too? Moe dozed.

Donnie laboured to help the other kids tramp out a big circle in the snow. They then etched out two spokes crossing through the centre. The reward for this hard work was a rousing game of fox and the goose. Snow tag games were popular, and this was the best. They laughed and played until melted snow soaked their woollen mittens and the cold bit through, freezing hands. The game flagged to a stop and Donnie fled home to the warmth of the big cook stove in the kitchen. His hands hurt and he buried them in his armpits until the painful tingle stopped. Many days like this were too cold to last long outside.

The ice rink gave an opportunity for many more tag games. They would make a complicated weave of paths on the snowy ice with the scrapers and then fly around on the trails with touch tag. Smaller kids like Donnie always felt disadvantaged.

Poison tag was the most fun, trying to catch someone while holding his skate heel. The rules said the tagged person had to keep a hand on the spot where another had touched them. It could be hilarious.

Perhaps the favourite game was shadow tag. At night, they would turn off the rink lights. A streetlight near the rink cast their shadows onto the surface. It tagged a person when the pursuer skated through their shadow. All of this made them excellent skaters with no lessons, bobbing, weaving, needing to take different poses with the poison tag and skating while squatting in shadow tag. The children lived in a glorious, unique wonderland that none of them appreciated.

"Shoot Donnie, shoot, you don't have a chance," Brian shouted from his goal crease. He wore the gear, while George, Curly and Jimmy tried to check Donnie.

"Here I come," Donnie broke for the net and let fly his best wrist shot. It caught Brian in the pads and bounced harmlessly away.

"Ha!" Brian yelled.

Donnie went to dig the puck out. George wore boots and Curly was not a good skater. Donnie would get a second chance.

If only I had a better shot, Donnie lamented. No matter how much coaching he got, he seldom remembered not to shoot right at the goalie. He was an excellent skater but could not play the game in his head.

Maybe Dad never told me to shoot at the post.

The hours they all spent in these endless games of shinny added up to fun, passing the long months of winter.

Donnie never felt the cold in his feet until he returned home and pulled his skates off. Two pairs of socks were not enough protection on most days.

Donnie is taking a shot
On the High Falls ice rink, about 1956. Brian Insley is in net. The others are perhaps Stanley and Curly Edwards and Jimmy Sutherland.

"Dad coaches John and me," Donnie said, "but I can't keep up. He once told me I was only playing to show off to the fans. I was, but Dad was the only fan I wanted to impress. I quit hockey after that year."

Moe stirred at Donnie's words, shifting for more comfort on the hard ground. The sound of vehicles below and shouting tickled his consciousness.

"I played once more, midget over age in 1963 to help make up enough teams in the league. Lots of games we only had five skaters and the goalie, and no coach. We made Chuck Ramsey our honorary coach. He had a bad leg and could never play, but he hung around the arena every day, smiling and joking with everyone. Dad didn't come to any of the games. Our makeshift team won the championship. Brian Insley played with us, and a kid from Espanola, Bruce Kennedy, who later joined the U.S. Marines and died in Viet Nam."

A coffee would kill this chill. Moe wiped a tear.

"Go to sleep, Donnie," Moe drifted into a more profound slumber.

"Steve," Corporal Sing's voice roused Warwick. "A couple of guys are here to check the dams."

Steve sat, blurry eyed and disoriented. It was near midnight. Sing offered him a coffee and Steve felt the warming tingle. They had a one-shot machine in the command van, and Steve guessed excellent coffee helped with many long hours in the field.

"The chopper will be here at first light. We'll call for the divers if they can't spot the guy." Sing sipped her coffee and eyed the cot. It would be her turn to catch a few winks.

Steve shook hands with the crew, experienced men who were part of the regular High Falls work gang. They knew more than he did about the work, and Steve squeezed into their truck as they drove up Big Eddy hill, around to the dam along the intake canal to No. 2 bulkhead.

"We'll do this one first," the lead hand said. "Check the upstream side. Most animal bodies float in there and don't sink into the racks."

The night was black, but the sky was a vast panorama of stars. Frost had not yet settled on the ground, but already the tops of the black railing pipes had a white sheen. With the turbines backed off, no sound came from the water that lay invisible against the dam. The workers shone a spotlight over the dark, still river but no sign of a body, human or otherwise. In no time, the trio was inside the structure, lights on and long-handled rakes disappearing into the water in the gap where the steel bars, space a few centimetres apart met the concrete floor. The men worked methodically each from opposite ends of the structure. They sank their long-handled rakes deep to the bottom and then pulled them against the steel trash bars and dragged them slowly to the surface. The wet handles glistened in the harsh light. Occasionally a bit of debris ended up wetting the floor, but in ten minutes, they finished the job.

"That's a relief," said the leader, "I hope No. 1 is clear too."

"So do I," Steve wanted to meet this Moe character.

An operation he had never seen before fascinated Steve. In No. 1 bulkhead, the layout was different, with the trash floor a meter or two below the entrance way and its concrete walkway.

"Damn," the lead exclaimed. "The controller hasn't backed off No. 3 turbine." He opened a call box and rang the direct line to the sub-station. Soon the two men were hard at work. There were four separate intakes here, and the process took much longer. These racks had more junk to pull out, but luckily, once more they did not find a body.

Everyone relaxed, and for the first time, had unstrained smiles.

"What do you think of the Wolves' chances this year?" The helper looked at Steve, perhaps hoping he would have someone new to talk hockey.

"They picked up that hot shot from the London Knights," Steve followed the sports pages but did not attend many games. "That should count for something."

"That's my hope," said the helper, "they sure need a winning season. The crowds are dropping off."

"The Espanola team has a chance in their league," the lead lived in Nairn Centre and followed his local teams.

"Yeah," responded his friend, "but they can only seat 400 in that fancy arena. That's not enough of a crowd to support a serious team or a higher league."

"They used to play hockey here," Steve thought of Moe's notes and photos. "Had a rink right about where the cops set up."

"A couple of my old retired neighbours grew up here," the lead said. "They tell stories. I'll ask about all that."

"Kids from here, when it was a town and from out the road to Turbine played here all the time."

Steve waited while the lead locked up the bulkhead. He leaned on the catwalk railing, over the faint glow of lights from High Falls No. 1 to the old town site, now lit by the security lighting on the power equipment and the activity around the police command post.

I wonder what it looked like at night 50 years ago.

A winter night from our backyard in December 1969

Whack, whack, whack

John and Donnie watched Dad swing his axe against the trunk of the aspen. It was about a foot thick and stood leafless and frozen in the still January air. It was cold, but not too cold, and the boys were more fascinated by the work than diverted by cold feet. Finally, the notch satisfied Dad.

"Move over there," Dad directed the boys. "The tree is going to fall in the notch's direction."

The wooden-framed Swede Saw came next, with Dad smoothly running his hand-sharpened blade through the soft green wood.

"Timber," he shouted, more in satisfaction than a need for a warning. The tree slowly toppled, twisting on the last bit of uncut trunk and then fell faster until it landed hard on some thick upper limbs. The sound of breaking wood ceased. Dad smiled.

"Stand back," Dad swung the axe, trimming the lighter branches quickly and then using the Swede on some thicker ones. He left a few of the bigger ones underneath, supporting the fallen trunk. The tree had made its sawhorse. Dad retrieved the two-man saw from the toboggan and took John to the log. He set the saw teeth onto the wood about a stove-length from the end.

"Pull, don't push, and don't push down on it. Let the weight of the saw do the work."

John got the hang of it by the end of the first cut. Then it was Donnie's turn. He was smaller and had trouble reaching for the proper angle. Dad occasionally looked frustrated but encouraged his younger son.

"Don't pull or push down on it. Now you're getting it."

Donnie smiled when the block dropped into the sawdust covered snow.

It took several trips to draw all the wood to the house, up past where Insleys docked their boat in summer and through the maples where the Haywards tapped maple sap in April.

"It fills the entire half of the woodshed," said Donnie.

"We never used much of that wood," Moe replied from his sleep. "Dad put it in as a back-up for the coal."

Donnie stood beside the flower garden and watched the man approach with a big bag of coal on his back. The man was short, swarthy but the black coal dust may have been most of his skin colour, and he walked as if the burden were no challenge at all. Donnie shuddered. He knew how heavy the coal was, having struggled with the scuttle from the bin to the kitchen.

Mr Taricani backed up to the side of the outside bin, its lid leaning high against the shed and spilt the anthracite over the edge. He had already filled the big bin inside the shed.

He headed back to his truck, parked about 100 feet away on the street with its box holding a depleting number of bags that he had filled at the depot, flashing a smile at Donnie, his white teeth brilliant against his coal-dust face.

Buying coal was a yearly ritual, every September for as long as Donnie could remember. Somehow, Donnie recalled, the siding at Turbine held a big car of coal for the town. Now, Mr Taricani brought it from Espanola. Either way, the stuff had ridden a train before it found the truck. It seemed like a tremendous amount of coal, „three tons Donnie' Dad said, but by May they would deplete it to a point where Dad probably worried they might run out. Of course, there was that dried aspen, just in case.

Dreaming of coal made Moe feel warm, he reached out, searching for Donnie's hand.

"Where are the infrared glasses? We can't search without them," Steve felt relief at not finding a body but frustrated with the lack of progress. Secretly, he blamed himself for not hurrying back to High Falls in the afternoon and getting Moe before there was a risk.

But I wouldn't know Moe, that way; Steve had found a good reason to feel better. *I wouldn't have found out about High Falls.*

"I don't think they'll help now," the incident commander laid a photo on the table. "We downloaded this satellite shot, here's the layout, and there are too many hiding spots. We are going to wait for daylight. It'll be," he consulted his watch, "about two hours. You might as well rest or go home."

"I'm staying," Steve said, "I feel this guy is a bit of a friend. His name's Moe, by the way."

"Maurice," said the sergeant, "we went to his motel. He had checked out, and he's alone. Our guys down south have visited his wife. I hope to have good news for her."

Donnie dug into the big snowbank created by shovelling the paths to the ash pile one way and the oil tank the other. It was always the biggest bank in the yard. He worked from near the hydro pole just above ground level, burrowing deep into the snow. Soon a small cave grew, and in no time he had a little chamber big enough to sit up in and turn around. It seemed safe enough. If it had collapsed, snow dust would have covered him and his legs buried, but his head would be in the open. He had read somewhere that Eskimos and natives travelling in winter would make burrows like this for a nighttime shelter on the trail. The whole thing felt as if it connected him to them somehow. If the dreaming turned to castles and armoured knights, and it were a snowy enough year, then he would dig upwards at the far end to make a little parapet like a medieval castle. He did not like that as much. It would lead to snowball fights with John and the others with the destruction of the cave and his little hideaway. Still, the work satisfied him.

Snowball fights were frequent, especially with the first wet snows of fall and in the massive deluge of white that usually marked the March lion. The late winter storm signalled the end of the ice rink since no one wanted to do the hard work of moving eight inches of wet snow. Mid-winter was too cold to compact the stuff into balls. Many handfuls of dry powder flew, and occasionally someone had their face washed, but mid-winter saw more tobogganing and skating than war.

Four of them sat on the toboggan. The heavier the riders could make it, the faster and further it would go, the scarier the ride. The faint voice of the friend watching for cars at the bottom sounded all clear, repeated by the mitten-covered hand of the relay at the mid-point curve. They pushed off the lip at the top and sped faster and faster, hitting the curve and its snow bank at a reasonable speed, riding high like an Olympic style bobsled. Screams and shouts filled the air with held breath. No one ever overtopped the bank. If they did, the cliff threatened on the far side; it was a ten-meter drop to unimaginable injury. Everyone thrilled at almost going over but hid their fear.

"Go, go, go...," cried the spotter who stood safely on the inside of the curve.

The sledge righted and headed down the main long drop, speeding to its next date with danger, the big bank behind the woodshed at what had been Grandpa's house where Tom Harley lived. Only a few ever went over the bank and crashed into the deep trench with a satisfying thump against the shed. They sped past the car-spotter and slid out towards the school, trying to reach Wiseman's before stopping. It was only possible when the sliding had turned the surface to ice. The four clambered off the toboggan and were ready for more.

"It's your turn to be the spotter, Donnie," Brian said. He prepared for the long, slippery trek back to the top of the hill.

Chapter Twenty

I awoke one day
In simpler times
The clang and clash long gone
My thoughts were of food
And fire and love
My heart was full of song.

The hill appeared as a dark grey shadow in the developing dawn. Steve sipped his fourth coffee and shivered. He had not dressed to spend a fall night in the open. Some of the jumbled weeds and grass shone a frost white in the mercury vapour lamps. The hum of the generator powering the police command truck was the only sound. By this time of the year, songbirds had fled, and it was not yet light enough to stir the crows and blue jays to complain.

"I think we'll find him somewhere up there," Steve nodded towards Big Eddy hill. "He came back down from the dam, but his tracks disappeared. The gravel is too stony, and the bit of asphalt doesn't help. It's easier to track a deer in the bush."

"You're a hunter," said Sing, making small talk. Hunting was not part of her family traditions, although she had a brother who went with his friends.

"Yeah, but this time I don't want to kill my prey. I don't even want to scold Moe. I want to talk."

"He's caused a lot of trouble and expense," Sing looked at Steve as if money summed everything up. Steve pulled Moe's notebook from his truck and showed it to the police officer. She read. Steve refilled their mugs.

"I only knew the city here in Canada," Sing looked up. "We came here when I was two. Dad and Mom talk about their home in India; they talk as this guy writes. I'll have to ask them more questions."

"That's how I feel too," said Steve. "I need to talk to my Dad."

"Warm sunshine," Moe stirred in a waking dream. Perhaps the chill was making him seek warmth, fishing in the sunshine, quiet, no worries, in a perfect world.

Dad rowed; Donnie sat in the back seat of the red, round-bottomed boat, enjoying the warm sunshine as Dad leisurely circled the No. 1 tailrace. Donnie's rod, the repaired broken one with the plastic cased reel, trailed a Canadian Wiggler deep beneath the surface. The fresh water, full of food from the bottom of the fore bay made this a productive fishing spot. Donnie and Dad had often fished from the concrete keeping walls along the raceway but seldom used the boat. It was too difficult when the turbines were on full power. With just No. 1 and No. 4 idling, the flow was easy for both boat and fish.

No 1 tailrace where Dad and Donnie fished

"I've hooked something," Donnie exclaimed, "but it is heavy and isn't moving."

"Must be a wire or something," Dad said. "Can you pull it up?"

Donnie drew the rod hard and reeled in the line on the down stroke.

"It's coming he said, but dead weight."

Donnie and Dad both watched the water expectantly, thinking they would soon see some debris thrown into the tailrace, the permanent garbage disposal for un-burnable stuff from the plant. It could be decades old.

When a faulty switch box had burned Grandpa Prentice and put into a six-week coma, Mom says the foreman threw the equipment in here before there could be an investigation. Maybe I've caught that, Donnie thought.

Suddenly, Donnie felt a wiggle and a flip, just as the yellow-white from the fish's flank flashed in the sun.

"A Pickerel," Dad exclaimed, "a big one." He readied the net and twisted for an angle, careful not to tip the boat.

The fish lay in the boat's bottom, entangled in the net with the lure lodged firmly on its gang hooks. It was the biggest fish Donnie ever caught. He usually caught two pounders that showed some fight. This old gal seemed resigned to her fate.

"Eight pounds," Dad stared at the scale in front of the washstand fish cleaning station, "almost as big as my record."

Dad had snagged a 12 pounder the year before, and his biggest fish was a 15 pound Pike that had taken 20 minutes to land.

Dad and his twelve-pound pickerel

The sun was about to peek above the horizon. Daylight had come, but not yet the warmth. Moe snoozed on, feeling Donnie's presence. When the drumbeat of the helicopter blades increased as the machine came up the valley, the sound stirred Moe. He opened his eyes and shivered. He was too cold and weak to sit up, so he lay beside the juniper bush, waiting and drifting in and out of wakefulness.

"Here it comes," Sing emerged from the command centre. Steve climbed out of his truck, and the party headed down the street that had a name for the first time, Hartman Street after the first superintendent. The machine rested on the gravel pad near the river, and the blades stopped rotating, allowing the dust to settle. The helicopter had no police markings. In Sudbury District, the budget only allowed for necessary rentals.

The sergeant spread the satellite photo on the ground, and the pilot and spotters squatted to follow.

The plan was simple. They would fly up Big Eddy road to the dam and pass around the structure a few times, circling the powerhouse and then the forebay, looking for…

"Probably a body," said the cop.

If they found nothing, they would pass along the river over the falls and rapids, which had a large amount of water flowing over, and down the near river shore to the lower powerhouses.

"If we spot nothing what do we do next? Cover that area west of these plants?"

"I don't think he's in there," Steve spoke up. "I looked hard, and no tracks went that way. The only tracks I saw were around Big Eddy. If anything, he's along the base of this hill." Steve pointed to the tree-covered hill to the north side of the site.

"We'll soon have the civilian volunteers for a ground search," the commander said. "A school bus load left Copper Cliff about a half hour ago. The dive team is on hold until after lunch. He could be a floater or stuck where the water is too dangerous for them. I've called for an ambulance, just in case, and a searcher could get hurt."

"We might have to stop wasting water," Steve said, "to dry out the falls so the ground guys can check." Steve did not relish telling his boss they would lose more production. The Ontario grid controllers would not like it. Only expensive natural gas generators could fill in.

"Okay, here we go," the pilot stretched. The crowd retreated, and the machine rose loudly, kicking up the dust and began its first run, a few hundred feet above the road and below the hilltop. The calm morning air made that safe.

"Donnie, did I ever tell you about the fires we made to sit around and chat in the evening?" Moe lay still, staring at the sky as it grew into a bright blue, wanting to be warm. The sound of the helicopter grew loud and then disappeared up towards the dam.

"We didn't need them for warmth, but I could use one now." Moe continued, despite Donnie's silence.

The kid must be asleep.

"It was the damned mosquitos," Moe wondered if he should swear in front of the kid, but he seemed to sleep, and these days kids heard swearing before kindergarten.

"The mosquitos here are ferocious after sunset. We needed the smoke to keep them away."

"Yes we do," Donnie finally stirred, "and we wear jackets done up to the neck and cuffs tied up too."

Moe smiled. The thought of fire made him feel warm.

"Brian Insley and I nearly burnt down the rink boards once. I bet I never told you that."

"We put the fire out and run up to the rock near the bridge," said Donnie. "It's always scary. I don't think anyone ever sees us."

Moe puzzled once more over the kid's penchant for making the past the present, and repeatable.

"Forest fires," Moe exclaimed a little too loudly. "They were scary. We only ever had two and an almost one. When I was a kid, some fishermen started one near the rapids. They put that out quickly." He wanted to see if the kid was listening, but Moe could not turn his head. He shivered despite the fire talk and laboured for a few breaths of air.

"The almost one was right down there, towards the school."

"Yes," Donnie sat up. "Right there," he pointed through the trees to a spot just a few meters away near the road. "The workers set their brush on fire, and it gets away the next day when they are gone. Our teacher sends my brother John, to raise the alarm. He talks to Gillis first, but Gillis says: „If a fire's there, someone wants it there.' Luckily John goes and finds someone else. They get the hose on it and stop it just before it goes up the hill. It would have burnt all this."

"Yes, he went to raise the alarm. That was the only time it ever happened," Moe sneezed.

"I could sure use a warm fire now."

Donnie did not reply. Moe fell asleep.

It took a half hour for the helicopter to complete the circuit and find nothing.

"Okay, Plan B", the police ground controller looked up at the circling machine. "Start out at the fence and fly right along the hill."

The machine swooped out over the river and came back in a long arc. If the crew had known Moe's High Falls, they would have realized they were passing over whip-poor-will rock. The thick bush and coloured leaves hid most of it. Just as they turned west, the ambulance arrived, followed by the busload of volunteers.

The vehicles pulled into the space in front of the command post. The paramedics tried to talk to the commander, but the helicopter had gone into a hover just above the command post, turning slowly about 30 meters above the lip of the hill.

The radio crackled, and the commander put his headphones over his ears to dull the noise.

"We found him," there was no excitement in the spotter's voice. "Right above you, about halfway up the hill. He's just lying there, not moving."

The commander's face fell as he relayed the word.

"He's been fifty meters from us all the time."

Steve reacted first, rushing to the hillside and working up the steep slope. There had once been a path here. He slapped the smaller trees aside and used the larger ones for handholds. The two paramedics were right behind him.

Moe lay under his silver survival blanket. It was the only reason he was still alive. Moe's cheeks were cold.

The paramedics shoved in, and Steve stood back, hoping.

"Is he alive? Will he make it?"

"Yes, to the first one," the medic said, "too soon to tell on the other, hypothermia."

Steve tore off his jacket and covered as much of Moe as he could. The paramedics did the same.

"It'll be hard getting him down that slope." The man shouted above the noise of the aircraft.

Steve called Corporal Sing. "Tell the helicopter to get lost, he almost shouted. It's driving us nuts."

The machine soon eased away and found its roost near the river. It seemed as if someone had lifted a weight from the scene playing out on the golden burnished hillside.

"It's flat that way, and the trees are thin," the medic was looking west along the old railway bed. "It looks like he came in there. Go drive the truck up the hill and bring the canvas stretcher. We'll have to ease him along there. Bring a drip."

It took twenty minutes before they could carefully place Moe onto the two-person carrier. The driver brought a third man to help, and they lifted Moe. The medic held an IV bottle high as they began their trek.

"Glucose and saline," he explained to Steve. "He's cold and dehydrated."

Moe turned his head and looked at Donnie. The kid walked beside the stretcher. The medics bobbed and dodged through the trees, but Donnie seemed to have no trouble as if the trees were not there, or maybe Donnie was not. Moe reached out and grasped Donnie's hand. He felt genuine enough.

"It's been nice meeting you, Donnie. It's as if I've always known you."

Steve reached for Moe's hand. The old man seemed to grasp for something. The weakness and the cold in the fingers shocked Steve.

"It's nice to meet you too, Moe. My name is Steve."

"You have always known me," Donnie smiled, and then looked sad. They eventually reached the ambulance, and the medics arranged the gurney where they would place Moe.

"I hope you keep enjoying playing here." Moe felt tired.

"I won't be playing here much longer," Donnie frowned, suddenly looking older than before.

"Why?"

"You're going."

"Yes, but you can keep playing. I won't tell."

"No, I mean you are going." Donnie's voice rose and sounded more mature. "When you are gone, I won't play here anymore. I won't need to play here anymore."

Donnie looked sad.

Moe sighed.

Donnie knew.

Moe knew.

It was impossible that one could know without the other.

Moe looked at Donnie; his eyes glistened at the sight of the young boy and the memories.

If we had only been us then…

Donnie's hand faded from his.

Steve released Moe's hand as the medics placed the gurney into the ambulance.

Steve dialled the security office.

"He's gone to the hospital," Steve knew Andrea would care. His sadness was deep. "It's touch-and-go. He has hypothermia bad and is rambling."

"I hope he pulls through," Andrea replied. "By the way, Pierre is going to give me a tour of High Falls next weekend."

"The first date?" asked Steve.

"Maybe," the answer was coy.

"How about we have a double date? Deb, I, and the kids can come. They need the tour too. You can come back to our place for venison chili." Steve partly wanted to be a catalyst for Pierre and Andrea. Pierre was shy, and too many poor relationships had hurt him. Steve and Debbie would grease the romantic skids if Andrea were as lovely as she seemed.

"Sounds good," she said. "Are you going with the ambulance?"

"No, they will let me know how it turns out. I'll visit the old coot in the hospital if I can. I want to talk to him."

Steve patted the notebook in his pocket. The photo album was in the truck. He would return it to Moe later.

"Let me know when I can visit him," Andrea rang off.

The ambulance cautiously backed down Big Eddy hill, and reversed in a hard turn towards the power plants, raising a slight moan from Moe. It then moved forward along the high road, heading to the gate along High Falls Road.

The old brown, weathered woodshed behind Albert Prentice's house passed to the right while the broken, grey rock that supported the old railway glinted to the left in the early sunshine. Walter Wiseman's red woodshed and shop slid by. Beyond the low road, the rink shack and the rink itself lingered in shadow while the tops of the four light-stands caught the sun above the rink boards. Steel footholds screwed into the poles to allow for lightbulb changing glinted in the light. Moe had never noticed that before. The ambulance crossed the concrete slab and approached the school. Mist swallowed the scene behind.

Moe felt the little jolt as the ambulance cleared the culvert.

Donnie ran through the sturdy red pines at the head of the island. His bare feet felt the soft brown needles that spread like a carpet. The sharp newer needles tickled his feet. The red pines stood in their glory, but somehow they were a chimaera, translucent, fading and wavering in his vision like a mirage. Donnie reached out to touch the red bark. It seemed to pass through his hand.

"I must get to the top," Donnie cried to the empty forest, "I need to see it."

He scrambled up to the top of the hill. The needles seemed less sharp now, and the rock not as hard. He stood looking over the forebay shimmering in the morning light, the deep red of Big Eddy powerhouse reflected in the surface and the whiteness of the dam in the background, but it all seemed unsubstantial, strange.

Donnie saw this from the top of the island

Suddenly, Donnie was at the top of the high hill, looking over the town. Briefly, it was solid, shining beneath an afternoon sun.

But it's morning, Donnie thought, n*ot, afternoon.*

There were the houses, the street with its crushed silica, the fire hydrant box, home free for hide-and-seek. Dad worked the garden, too far away for Donnie to hear the clack of his hoe. Lucky stood on the concrete walk at the back of the house, wagging his tail and looking up at Mom hanging washing on the line. An already full line fluttered in the breeze. The river ran deeper blue than the sky, with reflections of the dark spruce and white birch that hugged the far shore. The whistle blew from the plant, and soon several cars and a truck shot out the road.

Quitting time and supper will be soon.

Donnie looked to the town.

The scene faded, dissolving into a shimmering mirage of light and shadow. High Falls seemed to run away from Donnie's view, and darkness fell.

"No!" Donnie shouted. "We need more time."

The automatic gate slid shut, closing Moe off from High Falls.

For Mom on her passing

How many?

Walks on the Big Eddy Road
Workbooks of ours that you would hold
Showers in the pump room of old Number One
Blueberries picked in the afternoon sun
Dashes beneath the spraying log flume
Pansies and roses coaxed into bloom
Aprils with maple boiling, wonderful smell
Stories of the town would you tell
Pies and nappies and sealing jars
August evenings observing wonderful stars
Lessons of life often told
Stories from your memory all of gold
Baloney sandwiches at Clear Lake Beach
Sugar doughnuts, two for each
Fish and chips on the Little Current dock
Coal boats working around the clock
Times climbing Grandma's Wellington stairs
Aunts, uncles and cousins greeting at theirs
Fishing lines wet in Number Two race
Pickerel dinners right after grace
Games of five hundred, cards and all
Saturday dances at High Falls' hall?

Many memories from mind did fall
Because we thought them just too small
Things would we now give instead
To have these memories again in our head

-   *Don Hayward 2014*